UNDOCUMENTED

A Young Man's Quest for the American Dream

12/10/17

UNDOCUMENTED

A Young Man's Quest for the American Dream

To Jan + Jake our wonderful
friends for yours.
Enjoy!
In Czech love,
Adella

Adella Pospisil Schulz

Story Preserves, LLC
Denver, Colorado 80222

Library of Congress Number: 2017953097

ISBN-13: 978-1943324064
ISBN-10: 1943324069

Printed in the United States of America

www.storypreserves.com

This book is in memory of all the hard working ancestors, especially my grandparents and parents, who forged the way for those of us who followed. Their example helped pave the way for me and for my family, especially my brothers, sisters, cousins, my husband, our sons, daughters-in-law, and all of our grandchildren who every day know the value and satisfaction in a hard day's work whether it's at their job or in the classroom.

Czech Translations to English*

Ano – yes

Babička – grandmother

Buchty – deep-fried pastry with poppy-seed or other filling sprinkled with powdered sugar

Děkuji – Thank you

Houska – round roll pastry

Ja – I

Jezis – Jesus

Jitrnice – sausage

Kolache – National pastry with a dollop of fruit, rimmed by a puffy pillow of supple dough.

Kamos – buddy

Knedlicky – dumplings

Kočka – cat

Koruna – crown

Kyselé zelí – sauerkraut

Laska – love

Maminka – mom

Matka – mother

Milá – beloved

Milovat Ty – Love you

Muzika – music

Noc ~ night

Otcenas – The Lord's Prayer

Peníze - money
Pivo - beer
Pražské Noviny - *Prague News*
Rozumět - understand
Sestra - sister
Skr - cheese
Smetace - sweep
Srycek - uncle
Tá Naše Písnička Česká – beloved Czech song

Taroky - card game
Táta - father
Tetka - aunt
Veselý Doma - happy home
Voda - water
Zima - winter

*Translations from *Slovník*, English-Czech Dictionary, Czech-English Dictionary, New York, Hippocrene Books, 2003

Foreword

I have taken the real life of my grandfather, portrayed in this book, and have woven a fictional story around what I felt may have been his early experiences before the time I knew him. Any resemblance to actual events or persons, other than family members, living or dead, is entirely coincidental. Some of the events are real, while others are not. Only our family members will be able to discern the difference.

I hope you will enjoy the story I created as much as I enjoyed putting it into words for you.

One

His back and arms ached from a long, hard day at the coal mine in Kladno, Bohemia. The summer of 1885 was unusually hot. He lay atop his bunk hoping to fall asleep before it was time to get up to drag his young body back to the mine. As he moved his bunk closer to the window to catch a breeze, he heard voices from the garden below.

"I can't believe they actually saved up enough money to make the trip," his father was saying. There are nine of them going. You know one American dollar is 24 Bohemian Korunas and that would take 600 Korunas for each." Continuing to calculate, his voice raised as he said, "That would be 5,400 Korunas plus extra money they will need on the trip and after they get there. Where did they get that kind of money, Katie?"

Katerina replied, "Remember, Jakub, they've been saving a long time."

Franta wanted to shout out, "No, No, No. How can this be? His cousin hadn't said a word to him about their leaving for America."

He was riled with the news he had just over-heard. Sleep wouldn't come. *How I wish that our family was going. Why can't I convince Táta and Matka that we need to do the same?*

The next morning the sun streamed through the window as the rooster crowed the usual wakeup call, and Franta pulled on his soot-covered overalls ready to walk back to the mine for another day's work.

His mother had a lunch of fried pork sprinkled with caraway seeds, freshly baked rye bread, and one of her homemade dill pickles packed in an empty lard bucket that he and his father used as a lunch pail. *I am so sick of this life with coal dust all over me every day. It's in my hair, my eyes, in my nostrils, everywhere you can think of. Then there are the rumors of war. I'm not going to go fight so the Empire can take over more land. Wait until I get ahold of my cousin for not telling me that they are going to the new country. He won't have to work like a slave anymore with a new life on easy street.*

His cousin, Franz, who went by his middle name, Peter, was also nicknamed, Pepik. The cousin couldn't look him in the eyes the next morning. "You dirty rat. You knew all along and you didn't say a word. I thought we told each other everything!"

"You don't know how hard it has been to keep this secret, but *Táta* and *Matka* made me promise on the Bible. I don't know why this was so hush, hush."

It was June and their steam ship, The George Washington, would be leaving in the middle of August. Franta was angry. Angry that his cousin had kept this from him. Angry because he wasn't going too. He sulked about it most of the day. After a time he decided they would enjoy what time they had left together before the family left for America.

Peter and his parents, Uncle Thomas and Aunt Josefa, along with the other seven children visited his family often that month before they were to leave. Uncle Thomas tried unsuccessfully to persuade his in-laws to start planning to come, but Jakub always said, "Not as long as *Maminka* is still living. I can't leave her here alone."

So now the truth was out. It wasn't really a matter of not having the money like *Táta* had always led him to believe. *Now that I know that, I'm thinking differently. I'm going to start planning how one day I can go to America too. The entire family doesn't have to go. I can go it alone.*

Franta devoted all of his thoughts and schemes on how he would get to America. Going alone meant he would miss the smell of *kolaches* baking when he walked in from work, and there were those *jitrnice* his mother fried for breakfast. He would miss going to the tavern with his father to drink *pivo* and listen to the men talk and play cards. There was the accordion music and the polka bands they all loved to dance to. He enjoyed smelling the tobacco smoke from his father's ceramic pipe and yearned for the day he would have one too. He wondered how he could get along without his *babička* and his aunts, uncles, and cousins. Franta possessed a strong attachment to his homeland and to the earth, especially as he walked to work. He'd gaze off into the distance at the green, rolling hills wondering if there would be such land in America.

His parents moved to Kameny Most in the Kladno District of Prague (Praha) sometime after he was born in Caslava on August 8, 1874. His father worked in a shoe shop, but when he grew older, they moved to Kladno so his father could work in the mines and make twice as much money as he did repairing shoes. Franta worried about whether it was healthy for his father to work in the mine since he had heard others say men often died from black lung disease. And now that he was out of the required schooling, his body was as strong as that of any young man, so his father got him a job at the mine as well.

Franta asked himself, *Why is it that during the daylight hours, going to America sounds so exciting and when it's dark and I'm ready to fall asleep, it sounds frightening to me? I must quit thinking about it and just make a plan.*

August came too quickly. This was the day his aunt, uncle, and their family were leaving for America. His uncle had asked Franta to help them make the trip to the Port of Bremen, Germany. A train trip for his size family was costly and a boat trip on the Elbe was equally as expensive. The journey from Prague to Bremen would take a full day by horse and wagon. Thomas had it all figured out. Franta could help drive the wagon, and when they arrived, a livery would eagerly buy the horses and wagon. The sale would bring extra funds for the trip and enough money so Franta could take the train back to Prague.

"Here, Peter, I want you to have my warm coat. You will need this in the winter, and I can get another for myself at the St. Vitas bazaar."

"Are you sure? You are more like a brother than a cousin," Peter said.

The City of Bremen provided immigrant lodging for those waiting to depart. The family had never been part of such a large crowd before. There were upwards of 5,000 people waiting from all walks of life, speaking every imaginable language. Food was made available. It was a daunting experience for the ones like Peter's family who had never been far from their own community. They were, indeed, huddled masses.

Uncle Thomas, Peter, and Franta completed the sale of the horses and wagon. Franta was given his share of the proceeds for the train ride back home. However, there were no more trains leaving that evening. He assured his uncle that he would make out fine overnight with them so he could see them off in the morning.

There were over 500 people waiting to cross the gangplank onto the big ship, a North German Lloyd Steamship Line. As they loaded, it was mass confusion. All it took was to have your name on the ship's list. No passport, only identification was necessary for passage.

"It will take us two weeks or so to get there and when we do, I'll send you a letter to tell you all about the voyage," Peter told his cousin.

Just as he said that, his father was yelling, "Peter, hurry up and get in line so we can stay together." Franta watched as Peter hurried off and disappeared into the sea of people.

Since there is so much turmoil and no one is watching that closely, it wouldn't be hard to just slip on the ship without anyone even noticing, he thought to himself. *All I have with me is the badge from the mine with my name on it.*

Franta felt around in his pocket to see if the pocket knife and Korunas, along with his pocket watch, were there. He had also filled his pockets with raisins. He waited until the hundreds of emigrants had boarded and then made his way to an entrance he noticed no one else was using. He slipped inside of what looked to be a pantry with barrels of water and grain. He hid behind one of the barrels and said to himself, *I'm going to America.* Soon the sound of three loud blasts of the horn hung in the cool air and they were moving. He thought, *What can they do to me if they find me? They surely won't turn around for just one stowaway. I know Táta and Matka will be sad when I don't come home, but they will find the note I left on the feather pillow.*

He comforted himself knowing that he had left word so his parents would not worry about what happened to him. He must not think about his parents now, but instead, worry about how he would find his aunt, uncle, and cousins. As he hid behind the barrels he thought a lot about the large family he would be tagging along with. There was Peter, who is just two years older and his six siblings. So far, his scheme was working so he settled down on the wooden floor and dozed off.

The steamship left the port around nine in the morning. He was already getting hungry and the smell of food increased the gnawing. He must be somewhere near the galley. He stood up and stretched his legs, then carefully opened the door he had entered through. It opened up onto the deck and he saw no one around. They must all be waiting for food to be served. As he ventured out a bit farther, someone came up from behind him and said, "What are you doing out here, young man?"

"I got separated from my family. Can you help me find them?"

"Where do you think they are, first or second class?"

"No Sir, they are in steerage."

"Oh, I see. Come follow me."

The man with the ship's uniform led him below between the first class and second class floors to a space that was packed with people.

"This is steerage. Do you see them?"

After some pushing, shoving and searching he said, "Over there they are."

If the quarters had not been so crowded, his relatives would have dropped to the floor fainting away when they saw him.

"What are you doing here, Franta?" asked Uncle Thomas.

"I hope you aren't too mad at me, but I just couldn't let you leave for America without me."

Thomas turned to Josepha. "*Jezis*, Josie, what are we going to do with him? How are we going to get him through immigration without papers?"

"What will your *matka* say when she finds out what you have done?" she asked Franta.

Franta guiltily explained that he had left a note to his parents.

As the steamer continued on, Franta and Peter cowered in the corner. He bragged to his cousin, "Look at me, now. I am the one who kept the secret from everyone including you, my cousin."

Two

After the initial shock of discovering Franta, the family gathered their belongings and moved to a location Thomas staked out in the cramped quarters. They were allowed to have goose down pillows, clothing, comforters as well as some provisions of bread, salted-down pork, pickles and raisins. Someone advised Josie to bring along bars of homemade lye soap. It cured a variety of issues like sores, served as a disinfectant, and even kept lice away. The spot they chose was secured only by their sheer numbers as long as someone stayed with it.

Their steamer-trunk held clothing for the entire family, but Josie did manage to tuck in her mother's lace tablecloth and candle sticks so she would have something by which to remember her. Thinking ahead, Josefa saved cloth pieces and rags for months before the journey. Neatly folded pieces of cotton from yard goods and old tattered clothing would come in handy to dry off their faces and hands so as to keep clean and prevent skin infections. Rags for personal hygiene would be stored in a burlap bag to be laundered in America and would come in handy wherever they chose to settle. Thankfully, Josefa had toilet trained little Thomas so she didn't have soiled diapers to deal with on the journey over.

Rosalia overheard her parents talking. Wiping sweat from his brow her father said, "I still can't believe Franta had the nerve to run away like that. This is going to make our trip that much more difficult, Josie."

"I know, Thomas, but now that he's here with us we have to accept it and treat him as if he was part of our own family. God will see us through. Besides, you will have another hand to help out with the farming when we homestead in Nebraska." Josie said.

"There you go with your God talk again. I hope that God is on the other end holding out some cash to help pay for our nephew's keep," Thomas said.

"You know that won't happen, but God gave us all a mind and if we put it to work, we can figure it out. No sense in wasting our energy on anger. Besides, it makes everyone feel bad."

"Listen up, everyone," the ship's steward was bellowing. "These will be your daily provisions and make sure you don't waste any of them or you may regret it later. Each adult will get three quarts of drinking water daily along with bread, flour, oat-meal, rice, potatoes, peas, raisins, some pork, beef, fish, tea, vinegar, salt, pepper, and mustard. This will be your daily sustenance until we get to the port of Castle Gardens in New York City and what will be used for your meals. The ship is providing a tin washbasin, tin cup, plate, and utensils. There is also a pan to use for sea sickness. Each of you is assigned a numbered metal berth, a canvas mattress stuffed with hay, and a life preserver that you can use as a pillow. For those who need a blanket, notify me and I'll see what I can do for you. The children will get food and water apportioned according to their ages."

The steward also told them that he would need to see their ticket before he doled out their provisions. Thomas held the passage tickets, but he entrusted his wife to hold their other papers such as proof of inoculations, medical exam papers, and proof of haircuts and fumigation of their baggage. The officer reiterated that since they all had been vaccinated for small pox, the one main thing the Inspection Officers looked for was Trachoma, a disease of the eyes. "Immigration does not want people coming in with diseases, those who are not able to work, or those who are mentally unstable," he said.

"Well, I guess that leaves you out, Franta," teased his cousin when they heard the news about the mentally unstable.

"You're going to wish you hadn't said that," Franta said, jabbing Peter in the chest.

"Boys, stop that right now. There will be no horse play on board this vessel," Thomas said seriously.

"They're just having a little fun," Josie said to her husband.

"Is it okay with you if Franta and I go up on deck for a while to look around?" Peter asked his father.

"Don't be gone too long. We have to keep our space, you know, since we are all jammed in here like cattle under these six foot ceilings. There must be two to three hundred of us in this area."

Most of the other passengers were complaining about the deplorable conditions of the steerage section. Franta and Peter were young and adventurous so it didn't bother them.

The steamship made its way toward Liverpool that day. Franta and Peter were hoping they could keep track of how long it would take them to get there.

"I have some Koruna in my pocket. This is what I'll do. At the end of each day I will take one from the right pocket and put it in my left pocket," Franta said.

"Now isn't that a dandy idea!"

This first day proved to be exhausting for everyone in the family. They decided not to nap during the day regardless of how tempting it was to them so they could be assured of a good night's rest. As late afternoon approached, the cousins combed the deck, mostly trying to stay occupied and studying the ship's mechanisms as boys that age do.

"Do you see that man over there staring at us?" Peter said to Franta.

"He is giving us the evil eye for sure. Like we're doing something wrong. Let's move on before there's trouble," Franta suggested.

The steward in the steerage section announced to the mass of immigrants in their native language, "After I prepare the meals, you can eat at the tables over there, pointing to an area with wooden tables and benches, when your family name is called out. You each have your tin utensils with a tin washbasin, and a pan for sea sicknesses.

"Make sure you don't overeat so you don't get sea sick afterwards," Josefa cautioned the children.

She needn't worry about anyone overeating after they tasted what the steward had cooked for them. It had rice, potatoes and peas in it, but lacked any sign of meat for flavor.

"This looks like what *Maminka* used to feed her chickens," Franta said.

"I wouldn't be too picky if I were you, young man," Uncle Thomas said still roiling over the fact that he had one more charge to look after on the journey.

As the hungry, tired, and weary immigrants took turns with eating the evening meal, some of the older children were allowed to go on deck giving the rest of them some breathing room below.

"Just look at that sunset, cousin," Franta said to Peter, stroking his recently acquired chin fuzz. "I can't wait to see one when we get through the breakers and we're actually at sea."

As they made their way down below for the night, Peter pointed to the round holes he saw that had covers on them. "What do you think they are?"

"Let's find out," Franta said as he lifted the wooden cover only to discover the sea rushing below. "*Jezis*, someone could fall in and be swept away in the ocean," he said.

"I saw a guy squatting over one earlier. I'll bet they are privies," he said.

"We'll find out tomorrow after breakfast," Franta laughed.

"So much for any privacy, huh?" his cousin replied.

The young men felt it was their duty to explore as much of the steamship as they dared so they could report their findings to the family.

Three

Thomas and Josefa took turns sleeping so as to keep watch over their children, fearing the dangers of their conditions on the sea. By day, their oldest daughter, Rosalia watched over the three girls: Maria, age seven; Anna, age four, and Catharina, age three. Albert, who was eight, and his father's favorite, was looked after by his father. Little Thomas, stayed with his mother mainly because he was still nursing.

Considering their conditions and unfamiliar surroundings, the family rested as the steamship sailed her way toward the port in Liverpool. If it didn't get any rougher than this, they all believed they could manage the voyage, not remembering that they were on calm waters and that the turbulent Atlantic could bring about new perils and mysteries.

"I'm going to use the trunk as a table for the little ones," Josie said to Thomas. "We can use the *Pražské Noviny*, as a covering for the trunk. If you'll bring us some food from the mess hall, I won't have to subject the little ones to the congestion there with all the others."

Thomas was gone for quite some time and the children were getting fussy from hunger. Franta and Peter had gotten their rations since they were up early and in line.

As Franta heard the children whining, he moved closer reaching into his pocket. "Would you like a surprise?" he asked as he drew out four little black raisins from his trouser pocket. "Now, you must not eat your raisin right away, but instead chew and chew and chew until it melts in your mouth," he told them.

Josefa was touched by the way he pacified her little ones until Thomas was there with the oatmeal.

"Where did you learn to deal with little ones since you don't have any younger brothers and sisters?" she asked him.

"Oh, I just enjoy playing with them and raisins are a good way to do it," he replied just as their father came with their porridge.

Franta hurried off so as not to be in the way and also not wanting to hear any orders from Thomas. He knew he had more to do to get on the good side of his uncle. Peter and Franta slipped away to the deck once more, finding a spot away from the clamor of others as Peter pulled out a deck of cards from his pocket.

"Let's play some *Taroky*, huh, what do you say?" Peter said.

"We need four players though," looking around to see if there were any candidates nearby. "Why don't we see if Rosalia wants to play, and then we can ask that pretty girl over there to see if she wants to join us to make four," Franta said.

It took some persuading to get Rosalia to come up top with them, but her mother suggested she go with them to get some fresh air. The three of them were still in search of a fourth for their game. Just across from them the girl stood facing the outside with her head lifted soaking in the morning sun and early morning breeze.

"You go ask her," Peter said.

"No, you go. It's your deck of *Taroky*," Franta shot back.

Peter shuffled over and cleared his throat as he approached her. "Pardon me, Ma'am, we're looking for a fourth person to play cards with us. Would you like to join us?"

"Well, I may as well. There is nothing else to do on this filthy ship," she said.

"I'm Peter, this is my sister, Rosalia, and this is my cousin, Franta," he said.

"Hello, my name is Ludmila. My mother says it means gracious."

The boys looked at each other and swallowed their chuckle. "Do you know how to play *Taroky?*"

"Oh yes, doesn't every Bohemian know how to play that game?" she replied.

Time passed quickly as the four of them exchanged information about where they were from and where their families were heading. Franta had to be careful to not divulge too much information about himself. He knew he would be constantly looking over his shoulder for some time, but it would be worth it. Out of nowhere, his thoughts suddenly drifted back home to his parents as he wondered what they were doing at this moment and if they missed him. He would write when they got to America and maybe even send them some money after he got a job working for a farmer. Franta had read papers that the railroads sent advertising for free train tickets and jobs as farm hands in the newly formed state of Nebraska. He heard from others that there was land with rolling hills, much like the area around Kladno.

"Are you going to play or not?" Peter yelled at Franta.

Peter shuffled the cards for the deal and play began. Each player wanted to outwit the other and end up with the trump which was the *Tarok*. They went along chatting when all of a sudden Ludmila slammed down the trump. The rest looked at one another in amazement. They had seen men do that when they got the trump card, but never had they seen a woman smack the card down so forcefully.

"That's how my Dad does it when he gets a *Tarok*," she said. They were taken aback by her aggressiveness.

As they were playing cards, the boys noticed that the steward walked by and continued to leer at them.

A turmoil was brewing on the far end of the deck. Thomas came running, his eyes widened with fear.

"What's wrong, what's going on, *Táta?*" asked Peter.

"Albert is nowhere to be found. He was with me when I went after food and when I turned around, he was gone!"

"Oh dear God, don't let him fall overboard," Peter screamed out loud.

Everyone near them looked around sensing their panic. The deck was full of people. Some had come up to just stand and eat; others were already done. It would be difficult to spot an eight-year-old amongst the adults.

Peter and his family along with Franta spread out as much as they could, looking for their little sibling.

"If he is lost, Josepha will never get over it," Thomas wailed.

"Don't worry, we'll find him," Franta said to his uncle.

They did the best they could but no sign of the youngster. A flash came through Franta's mind as he quickly charged through the crowd, bumping into elbows and causing a couple of food pans to go flying.

"Watch where you're going, you ruffian," one man shouted.

It seemed like forever until Franta reached his destination. There, lying over one of the privy holes was the eight-year-old Albert, flat with his belly on the deck simply watching the water as the ship rolled over the sea.

Franta calmly came up alongside of him. Albert looked up upon seeing the grey pant leg next to his head, Franta shouted, "Don't move!" Bending down, he swooped Albert up and looked around for the lid to cover the hole.

"*Jezis*, kid, what do you mean wondering off like that? You could have fallen in," Franta scolded.

As soon as he did, Albert began crying and everyone was looking at Franta as if he was beating him.

"I didn't mean to scare you. You're okay. I'm just happy I found you and that you're safe."

That was a close one, Franta thought to himself as they walked back below only to find Aunt Josepha sobbing. Albert ran to his mother for consolation. The rest of the family scurried to their cramped quarters.

Josepha motioned them all to go, leaving Albert, Little Thomas and her alone with their father, more than likely, to soften the wrath of her husband toward Albert's disappearance. They heard her tell her husband, "Go easy on him, Thomas."

Four

Little time was spent in the Port of Liverpool as passengers were not allowed to disembark. Word had gotten around that crossing the breakwaters could be rough. Josefa prepared her family by rationing their meals before they set out. She had also brought along mint leaves for them to chew on should they feel queasy. The family matriarch did her homework that proved successful for her family, but others were not so lucky. The jousting and lurching of the ship was more than many could handle. What made it difficult was that watching others wretch, and smelling the stench was more cause for sea sickness than the rough waters. Thomas and all but Josefa and little Thomas chose to go on deck even though it was cold and wet. At least they didn't have to endure the sights and sounds of the shipmates.

"Whew, that was a rough ride, eh, Franta?" Peter called out as they were finally out on the murky, green Atlantic.

Josefa praised her children and Franta on how they handled the rough waters. "You listen well – a valuable lesson to you when we get to America and have to set out to work. Your father will need all the help he can get after we reach our homestead."

Most of the remaining days at sea were a repeat of what they experienced in the days prior except for the breakwaters. The children played games with the older ones and Franta continued to play cards whenever he could find willing partners. Thomas and Josefa read the publications they brought along.

"Everything is going well," Thomas said to Josefa.

"I haven't wanted to say anything, but I need more drinking water as it seems that my milk is drying up and I don't want little Thomas to go without. This is not the time to be weaning him."

Franta heard them talking and said to Peter, "I know where I can get them water. Just wait until tonight. You must come along to be my lookout, though."

The boys waited until after the evening meal was over, and the stewards were busy with the first-class passengers, to make their water run.

"What will we carry it in? Peter asked."

"We will use the tin pan they gave us for sea sickness. If we get caught with it, we can say that we came on deck to use it so the family wouldn't have to listen," Franta said.

"How about if we're caught with water in it, then what?"

"Let's not worry about that now. Let's just make sure the light is just right. Okay?"

Franta remembered where the storage area was where he had hidden when he first got on board. He remembered there were barrels of water and other provisions there.

The lights had just been turned on in the upper decks when the boys set out on their water heist. They walked up to the deck as they had days earlier. Their watchful steward seemed to be nowhere in sight.

"You stand as lookout for me when I go inside this door," Franta told his cousin. When I have a pan full of water, I'll clear my throat twice to let you know I am coming out."

"If anyone is watching, I'll clear my throat three times, so you stay in there longer," Peter told him.

"Okay, here goes," Franta said as he lifted the lids on the wooden barrels. Not in this one, nor this one or the next, he thought as he lifted one after the other. At last, he found the one that contained water. He filled the pan as high as he dared so it would not spill and remembered to put the lid back on the barrel. *Now all we need to do is get back down below deck.* Franta was like his father and not particularly a religious young man, but this time he made the sign of the cross thinking of his *maminka* and remembering that she taught him to pray.

Did I say I would clear my throat twice or three times? He thought amidst his anxiety. *I think it was twice.*

Franta listened closely, but didn't hear the reply they agreed to. He waited and waited. Franta cleared his throat twice more. Still no reply. *The coast must not be clear. I will wait.* He waited and waited, but still no response. *Wonder what is going on out there?*

At last he heard the three "ahems" from his cousin. The deck was okay. The door to the storage opened. Peering over Peter's shoulder was the cross eyed steward.

"So. What are you doing here, young men?" the Steward quizzed.

"I am stealing water for my aunt who doesn't have enough to make milk for her baby," Franta said.

"That's the most honest answer I've heard in a long time. Go ahead. Go. If you need more for the baby let me know. My wife and I just had a baby two months ago."

Franta and Peter couldn't believe their ears. Here was a man they thought was their enemy and it turns out he was on their side.

Maybe that little prayer helped after all.

Five

Franta and Peter heaved a huge sigh when the steward moved on. They carefully made their way back to the family.

"What do you boys think you are doing roaming around the deck after dark?" Thomas asked. Then he saw the pan of water.

"We know that *Maminka* needs water and Franta remembered where he could get some. Don't be upset with us. We are only trying to help," Peter said to his father.

Thomas was visibly moved as he watched Franta fill their other containers with the water they had pilfered. "That was a very kind act, boys. What if you had gotten caught?" he said.

"We did," Peter said. "Franta just told the steward the truth and he understood."

Next morning when they were being served breakfast, Thomas came back to Josefa wearing a wide smile on his face. "Look what I have for you," holding out an extra cup of water. Steward says that this is for you and the baby. "We have Franta's courage and caring to thank for that," Thomas said.

The days seemed less strained between Uncle Thomas and Franta after that. "I think I've finally proven myself as a worthwhile person," Franta told his cousin.

"How many coins are left in your pocket?" asked his cousin.

"I have two left so if they are on schedule, we should be there day after next." Franta said.

The family busied themselves with the usual games and reading as they had done all along. How glad they were they had not encountered rough seas as when they crossed the breakwaters at the beginning of their trip. If the waters leaving the harbor were rough, they wondered if entering a new harbor would have the same effect. They agreed that the voyage was not nearly as difficult to endure as the terrible food which consisted mostly of stew or soup made from their provisions.

"I will never complain about food ever again," Young Albert said.

Six

Family spirits were high with the journey approaching its destination into New York Harbor.

"Come here, boys, I want to show you something very special," Thomas said to his son and Franta. The sky was without moonlight that night causing the stars to hang brilliantly. "Look up there," pointing at the North Star. "If you ever need to find your way at night, just look for the Polaris and it will be there to guide you."

Thomas was relaxing some now that they were about to reach America. He had taken on a new demeanor after the water episode a few nights earlier. Franta was relieved to not have his Uncle's anger weighing on his shoulders. He would wait and see how long the new attitude lasted toward him.

A low murmur from those left on the deck that night reached their ears. "Wait, do you hear that?"

Neither of the young men could discern where the music was coming from. It sounded very much like someone was playing *Tá Naše Písnička Česká* while others around the accordion player were singing in unison. Was this just a figment of their imagination? Maybe their minds were deceiving them like those of weary travelers across a desert who see a mirage. Why did the musician wait until now to play? Everyone could have used the music days ago when their spirits were low. The words about a Czech song brought a twinge of sadness to Franta's heart. It took him back his parents, causing him to wonder if they missed him as much as he missed them. He could not allow himself to go down that emotional path.

"Let's go see if we can find the accordion," Peter said to Franta. He sensed his cousin's melancholy. "They should be singing some American songs now that we are so close to arriving."

No more had he lamented those words when the English speaking passengers began singing *My country 'tis of thee, sweet land of liberty, of thee I sing.* Even though the cousins did not understand the words, the melody captivated their ears.

"When I have sons, they will play that song on their musical instruments. I will make sure of that," Franta said.

With the music in the background, they heard a group of men talking about the Statue of Liberty they would be passing by in the New York harbor on their way to Castle Gardens.

"I read in the newspaper that France gave the gift to America and when it arrived in June of last year, it was in 350 pieces," one man said to the other. It took 214 crates to get it there. Then they had to hire workers to put it together and build a base for it to sit on."

The other man replied, "I wish I could be there when they dedicate it this October, but I can't wait around that long before we go west."

Peter and Franta always did enjoy sitting around listening to the older men talk. They could learn so much from them. When the music stopped and the men broke up, the boys headed back to their family sleeping quarters totally unaware of the day that lie ahead.

Seven

It seemed like any other morning yet there was a strangeness to the air. Even the fish that followed the ship were acting strange. Suddenly a gust of wind swooped through the deck. They heard yelling and saw many passengers scrambling to get to their quarters.

Peter and Franta ran to see if they could find Steward to see what was going on. "Get down to your quarters," he shouted at them. "We're in for a tropical storm."

"Is it a hurricane?" Franta shouted back.

"No, Captain has equipment now days to stay away from those, but we're getting the downward side of the hurricane. Hurry, get down with your family!" he barked.

They were using all their might to stay upward. "I can't believe how quickly this came up," Peter shouted.

"I can't hear you. Let's get moving."

"Look, there's that guy's accordion. It's going to get ruined. I'm going after it," Franta yelled.

"No, leave it there. It's not worth risking your neck for," a frantic Peter called out.

Josepha beamed when she saw Peter come down. "Where's Franta?" she asked.

"He went after this guy's accordion," her son replied.

The wind was picking up velocity, bouncing the ship around like a cork in a tub.

"Why didn't the captain steer clear of this?" Thomas lamented.

"Steward said it's the tail end of a hurricane. Maybe it snuck up on them."

The family huddled together riding out the waves. If only Franta would get back down here, Josepha thought.

"I told Franta the accordion wasn't worth risking his life for, but he did it anyway," Peter told his parents.

They had read and heard of ships being lost at sea, but could this be happening to them? "I don't want our family to drown at sea," Josepha cried out.

The hatch to their area burst open as together Franta and another man came staggering in. *What's he doing bringing someone else down here? We hardly have room as it is*, Thomas thought.

Three-year-old Catharina cried out, "Look, 'cordian."

The beautiful four-row diatonic button accordion was spared the ravages of the rain on deck, thanks to the quick thinking of Franta.

"Listen, everyone. This is Joe. He's going to Nebraska to farm too. We're going to be neighbors one day," Franta told them.

The steamship continued to churn and roil, but she seemed to be weathering the storm.

"Play us a polka, Joe. We need to think about something happy," Franta said to him.

Joe obliged by playing the tavern song, "*Já Ráda Tancuju*," I'd Like to Dance.

A nearby passenger heard them singing and said, "I'd rather be dancing too."

Eight

As quickly as the winds came up, they blew out to sea in the opposite direction. The steamship wasn't far out now. They could tell by all the birds that were circling the ship. They also noticed the clouds building up in the distance signifying there was land ahead.

"Now, if some of you will go up above, I can have room to get our things together in preparation for arrival," Josepha told her family. "There will be a lot of milling around and everyone will be in a hurry, but remember, family, we must all stay together. This will be a very busy place, and we don't need anyone getting lost and complicating things," she said.

Excitement filled the air with energy as everyone looked forward to finally reaching their destination of Castle Gardens, New York, on September 7, in the year of 1885. They were able to all move up on deck as Thomas and the older boys carried their belongings with them. They got an early start so they would be sure to all see the harbor as they entered.

"Look, look, everyone. There's the Statue of Liberty welcoming us to America," Rosalia announced as they sailed by.

Peter and Franta tried their best not to let their emotions show as their chests filled with joy and their eyes held back tears. America at last!

"Move right up this way," the man in a uniform motioned them to get in line.

"What are we going to say if they question why Franta is an extra?" Thomas asked his wife.

"Let me handle it," she said.

They inched their way through the line where the doctors checked them for lice. No problems there. They moved to the next line where they checked their eyes for trachoma. No problems there either. As they approached the line where the passenger lists were being checked, Josepha whispered to Little Thomas to play hide and seek with her in her long, billowy skirt.

"Let's see, there are nine of you in your family, is that correct?" the Uniformed Man asked.

"That's correct," Josepha replied, struggling to keep the passenger list from shaking in her hands.

Just as this happened, a skirmish broke out nearby and the Uniformed Man was being called over to help out. He waved them on through. This was the last line they needed to go through before they could set foot on American soil.

The Jelineks and their stow-away nephew made their way outdoors onto what appeared to be a circus. Lining the walkways were vendors selling everything from fresh fruit to clothing and tools. If the immigrants had the money, it was there to be spent. Off to one side was a booth where they could exchange their money for American dollars. Franta was eager to swap those Korunas he had so carefully switched from one pocket to another on the voyage. Off in the near distance he heard a musical melody. Eager to check it out, he started forward and remembered that his Aunt Josepha had warned them all to stay together.

"Peter, I need to see where that music is coming from. Ask your *matka* if we can walk in that direction," he said.

With their currency exchange out of the way, they made their way down the walkway. A vendor was selling harmonicas that Franta felt looked easy enough to play. Franta only knew a few words of English, but fortunately, the service providers had been working with immigrants for many years now and most of them had learned crucial words in German, Czech, Polish, and other languages of immigrants.

"That will be five cents," the man said as he let Franta take his pick.

Franta was thrilled beyond measure. This would give him something to do on long lonely nights.

Thomas stopped and asked the family to wait for him as he inquired about a reasonable place for them to sleep that night. They could all use a good night's sleep. That done, they followed the instructions given him to find a boarding house not many blocks away.

They were still trying to get their sea legs on land as they walked and the children were asking for food. They yearned to sink their teeth into fresh fruit.

"Oh, Thomas, can we afford to buy an apple for everyone?" Josepha asked.

"The man said they would feed us at the boarding house this evening, but, yes, we all need something and an apple sounds the best," as he doubled back and bought ten apples. They found a grassy area and sat down munching on the best apples any of them had ever eaten in their lives. Even little Thomas was ready for some food he could sink his teeth into. They all complained about the awful food they had been served aboard ship.

"Oh well, we didn't starve, did we?" Franta said.

"Doesn't he ever get sick of being so positive?" Thomas said in a low tone to Peter.

The family kept close to one another so as not to become separated in the masses of people strolling around the streets. The tall buildings were the most intriguing to them all. Thomas had the map drawn out for him along with the name shown on his list. After walking several blocks, Rosalia called out, "The big house has a sign that says, Veselý Doma. Is that it?"

Their father said, "That isn't the name the man gave me, but let's stop and see if they have room for us."

Nine

"Welcome, welcome," the little rosy-cheeked lady exclaimed in Bohemian. "Look at you all. You must need a place to spend the night before you head to Jersey City to catch the train."

"Why yes," Thomas said. "But how did you know?"

"That's what all the families do when they come to America. Where are you folks headed?"

"Nebraska," Josepha replied. "We are looking for quarters for all ten of us along with some supper. Can you take us in?"

"Some of the children may need to sleep on the floor, but otherwise I will happily make you some supper. I also, have a bath tub and running water, so you can all take a bath after you eat. That's why I called my boarding house, Veselý Doma, or Happy Home, to accommodate the Bohemian families coming over. You know I was in your shoes once too. A kind lady took us in, and when she passed on, I took over her rooming house. Now, do you all like potato soup?"

"We will be grateful for anything you fix us," Josepha said before anyone else had a chance to reply. "Show us the way and we will start cleaning up."

Thomas and the boys carried the steamer trunk up the stairs. At last they would be able to get out of the clothing they had worn across the Atlantic. All except, Franta. He had no extra clothing.

"If anyone in your family is in need of clothing, there is a Salvation Army Store not far from here. They carry clothing for little or nothing. It is within walking distance and easy to find," Miss Ruziicka said.

"Let's get the directions, Peter," Franta said to his cousin. "I need another change of clothes. I will have to part with some *penize*, but that is how it is."

When the boys reached the store, Franta noticed the floor needed sweeping. He knew some English from primary school, so he approached the lady dressed in a grey uniform standing behind the counter and said, "Ma'am, Clothes? *Ja smetace.*" He motioned to himself doing a sweeping motion and then pointed to the clothes.

"*Ja rozumĕt.* I understand," the lady said. She was used to dealing with immigrants from Europe who had limited English as so many of them came through the store. She motioned for them to wait as she called the manager out. She whispered something to him as the boys waited anxiously to see what he would say.

She got the okay from the manager and both Franta and Peter went to work cleaning the store.

The cousins had little trouble finding something for Franta to wear. They wondered where all the clothes came from, but kept their thoughts to themselves and each grabbed a broom. The store was much bigger than it looked and it took them some time to get the job done. The uniformed lady wrapped the clothing in brown paper and tied it with string, and the boys went on their way.

"Those boys are going to do well in America," the manager said to his employee.

The shadows were beginning to grow long, and there was but a glimmer of sunshine left on the horizon as the boys made their way back to the Veselý Doma.

"Where have you been? We were beginning to worry that you got lost or mugged!" Thomas said.

Peter took over the answer and explained how they earned the clean, used clothing for Franta and how it was an offer they couldn't pass up.

Not only could they smell the aroma of the potato soup, but freshly baked bread permeated the air. *It was almost too good to be true*, Josepha thought. *Will everyone be this nice in America?*

As the family sat down at the boarding house table, Thomas raised his right hand to get their attention. "Your Mother will say the blessing tonight," as they all made the sign of the cross. "Let us also give thanks for our safe journey free of sickness. May God continue to bless us. Amen." They all dug in.

They took turns bathing with the youngest first, and the rest followed up through Uncle Thomas, who bathed last. How good they all felt letting the grime roll off their bodies. Getting their hair washed felt equally refreshing. They had been assigned their quarters by Miss Ruziicka. The older ones bunked down on the third floor on cots. You could tell the lady was no stranger to accommodating incoming countrymen. As they settled in, Franta turned to Peter next to him and said, "I'm wondering if we could stay here another day and night."

"I don't think *Táta* will go for that," Peter said. "Why would we want to anyway?"

"I'm wondering if the opportunity to work for clothing will ever come up again before we reach

Nebraska. I need heavy winter clothing and where else am I going to get it?"

"I guess it won't hurt to ask," Peter said as he rolled over to get some sleep.

It was the first time in over two weeks that the family had slept soundly without the pitching and heaving of the steamship. They awoke rejuvenated as they dressed for their second day in America. Miss Ruziicka made coffee, oatmeal and more freshly baked bread. Josepha knew her last day of feeling pampered was about to come to an end. Then something unexpected came about.

Ten

"I don't know if you would consider staying on another day and night," Miss Ruziicka said to Thomas at breakfast. "There is no end to the work I need done around here, and you all are so helpful with Josepha and Rosalia and their kitchen skills. Thomas and your boys could chop some more wood and stack it. I have miscellaneous work outdoors before winter sets in. What do you think?" she asked.

"Before you make up your mind, Uncle, I was going to see if I could go work at the Salvation Army long enough to earn a warm winter coat and galoshes. I hear the winters can get mighty cold in Nebraska," Franta said.

"Josepha and I will discuss this offer after breakfast and get back to you soon," Thomas told the Innkeeper.

It left one problem, however. How could Franta help out both at the boarding house and still have time to go to the Salvation Army to earn clothing. Time was of the essence. The clothing store would not open until nine o'clock and they closed at six. That left two hours he could work here and hopefully, if he worked hard and fast he could get back by four in the afternoon and still have daylight to do what more needed to be done. Franta waited eagerly to hear their decision.

"My wife and I have decided to take you up on your offer. However, one of our boys can only work part of the time during the day because he needs to earn money for clothing at the Used Goods Store. We will finish whatever you set out for us to do since you have been most generous and kind to our family," Thomas said to Miss Ruziicka.

She agreed and both Franta and Peter hurried outside to begin their chores. The women-folk took to their duties in the kitchen with washing dishes, scrubbing the floor, others cleaning the bathroom upstairs and Josepha started a batch of bread. It delighted her to be back in the kitchen again as she dreamed of the house they would have one day in their new land.

"Miss Army," Franta said to the uniformed lady at the store. "Ja need clothes. Zima." He hugged himself like he was cold. "More work. please?"

"We just got a wagon-load of donations that need sorting," the Miss said. "Do you think you can do that if I tell you what I want done?"

"*Ano, Ano,*" said Franta and nodded his head up and down vigorously.

Franta's stomach began to growl as it approached lunch time. He hesitated to use his newly exchanged American money for food yet he needed something on his stomach.

"*Ja go Veselý Doma?* Get food. Come back fast," he said to Miss Army.

"That won't be necessary, young man. I have an extra egg sandwich in the back. Let me get it for you."

The sandwich stopped the growling in his stomach and even though he could have eaten another one, Franta made do and busied himself with the sorting. He came across a sheepskin coat that fit him a little loosely, yet that way he was able to gain back the weight he had lost on the way across. He found a pair of five-buckle rubber overshoes and a woolen cap that had flaps to come down over his ears. Now all he needed was some underwear and gloves. He worked fast as if looking for treasure. In a sense, it was treasure to him. Then he remembered he would need a satchel to put the clothes into since it was just the beginning of autumn and not yet that cold out. By the time he unloaded the wagon and set things out, he had found woolen gloves, but the most prized find was a grey felt homburg hat.

When the time came to settling up for his purchases, Miss Army rang them up. Not understanding the American monetary system yet, he noticed the look of dismay on her face.

"When I tally up your work hours and the amount for the clothing, you come up a little short," she said. "It's the hat that puts you over the top."

His forlorn look tugged at her heart and she said, "Oh, go ahead and take it anyway."

"*Děkuji*, Miss Army, thank you. Bless you on *Matka's* heart," Franta said.

As he stuffed the boots and clothing into the satchel, Franta made his way out the door feeling like skipping, yet thinking it would be inappropriate for someone five feet ten inches tall to be acting in such a childlike manner.

That night as he lay his head down to sleep, for the first time in many months, he said a prayer of thanksgiving and thought about his mother and father back in Kladno. He was somewhat relieved that no one questioned that he was undocumented. Nevertheless, he would always have to be careful and not give too much information away so he wouldn't be sent back. Franta's new found religion gave him pause.

Eleven

Early the next morning he asked Miss Ruziicka, "Do you have a sheet of paper and an envelope? I need to write to *Maminka* and *Táta* to let them know I'm safe.

She felt a sudden pang in her heart thinking of what it must be like for his parents to have let him come so far away alone without them. Little did she know, as she produced a lined piece of tablet paper, envelope and even a postage stamp, that he had stowed away without them knowing it. He felt no point in telling her either. His letter, of course, was written in his native tongue of Bohemian also referred to as Czech sometimes.

Draho Maminka a Táta ,

I hope you have not been worrying about me. I am sorry I left so suddenly, but there was no other way for me to do it since I hid on the ship to get free passage. I figured I wouldn't be noticed since

I joined up with Tetka and Srycek. The crossing went well for the most part. The food was terrible and I lost some weight, but now it's better.

We saw the Statue of Liberty two days ago for the first time. A nice Bohemian lady let us stay in her Boarding House in exchange for work. She told us where to go to get used clothes. It is called the Salvation Army. Miss Army at the store told me they have been around for over twenty years helping immigrants when they come here.

I miss you and am hoping for the day when you can come to America to live. I have my eyes set on land called Nebraska. It is to be somewhat like the land near Kladno. Please don't worry about me. I am doing fine. Thank you both for teaching me how to work. It is helping me get to where I want to be.

I will write again in about a month after I am settled in my new territory.

Milovat Ty,
Franta

Twelve

Leaving the letter on the library table for mailing, Franta ran upstairs, two steps at a time, in order to use the bathroom before they left the house.

"Hurry up in there," he said as he pounded on the door knowing that Peter was occupying it. "The troops have sounded which signals the army is on the way," he added knowing that his cousin knew what that meant. Franta often used double talk to get his point across that had an edge of humor associated with it.

All their belongings were packed once more and the steam trunk was carried downstairs. Everyone seemed refreshed and ready to embark on their next leg of the journey westward. The autumn leaves crunched beneath their feet as they made their way to the barge that would take them to Jersey City to catch their train to Nebraska. Even as early as they were, the line for tickets was lengthy. Franta told his uncle he needed to go up to the ticket window to get some information. Thomas thought little of this since Franta was known for his enterprising spirit. After reaching the ticket window, he motioned to the matron at the window to open the door that entered the building. She obliged and he walked in as though he belonged there. A uniformed man stopped him shortly and asked him where he was going.

"I was told to see the captain of this vessel about working for my passage to Jersey," he told him.

"Wait here, young man, he's right over there," motioning him to walk on over.

Franta greeted the captain with the tip of his grey felt homburg hat he got at the Salvation Army.

"What is it young man?" the Captain asked.

"No money. *Ja* work for trip? Take tickets?"

"You are mighty courageous to ask, and we need people like you in this country who are willing to pull their weight. Sure, go stand over there and when the first passengers come on board, unhook the rope and tear the stub off their tickets. Put the ticket into this bucket and give them their portion."

"*Ja* tell *Strycek*," Franta said. "How *Ja* come back here?"

The Captain reached into a compartment behind the cabin and pulled out a cap. "Here, put this on to let our people know you belong inside."

Franta wanted to skip out to the line waiting outside, but thought better of it as he walked through to where they were waiting and told them he had a job taking tickets.

"I'll see you when you pass through," he told them.

"You are one brave guy," his cousin said to him.

"I have to be. I don't have a father with me to pay my way."

He picked up the satchel with his clothes, plopped the barge cap on over his Homburg and marched back in through the door ready to go to work.

The vessel made its way delivering a load of immigrants, including the Jelineks, to the train station in Jersey City, a popular place for those making their way west to new frontiers. Franta made sure the tickets he collected were in the hands of the purser before he disembarked. He would have to find a way to reach the railroad engineer to see about working his way west to Chicago. There they needed to visit Cousin Adolph and his sister, Rose.

It was Adolph and Rose that Thomas and Josepha listed as the family's sponsors. By doing so, it provided the United States Government a way of tracking the influx of new people and in addition showing federal officials that someone who had already been living in the country was vouching for them. Even though Franta had no documentation to this effect, he was somewhat immune because he was traveling with the family they assumed he belonged to.

"Well, wish me good luck," Franta told the family as he wended his way through the masses and over to the ticket window once more.

He repeated what he had done on the barge and wearing the cap he was given, Franta searched behind the scenes for someone who looked as though he might be the conductor.

"Do you need help taking tickets?" he asked the uniformed man standing on the platform.

"Sorry, son, it's a one-man job and I have it covered," the conductor replied.

My luck is about to run out, he thought to himself just as the conductor yelled at him to hold up.

"Go up to the engineer and see if the fireman needs someone to help him shovel coal," the man said.

Franta hoisted himself onto the big black iron horse that bore the No. 89. He made his way to the front.

"Ahem," he went to the man wearing bibbed overalls and a cap with the initials, UPRR.

"What do you want?" the Engineer said gruffly.

"*Ja* work coal mine in Bohemia. *Ja* shovel coal." He motions shoveling coal. "Stoker? No *penize*. Go to go Nebraska."

"It's a hot, dirty job, but you can give my fireman a hand. He takes orders from me to keep the steam gauges at the proper levels. Stay around, son. He should be here before very long."

Once more, Franta asked the engineer's permission to notify the family what he would be doing so as not to worry them. In addition, he didn't want his uncle nosing around supervising him.

I have jumped another hurdle, he thought to himself. *This job isn't going to be as easy.* He reminded himself of all the coal he had shoveled in the mine at Kladno. *It can't be that much different.*

The mighty No. 89 chugged away from the depot on a journey that would take them the greater portion of two days traveling at about 45 MPH through Pennsylvania, Ohio, and Indiana before reaching Illinois.

With every clickity-clack of the railroad track, with every chug-a-chug-chug of the steam engine, Franta shoveled coal into the firebox. As the Pennsylvania Railroad locomotive began its assent up a steep grade through the mountain terrain, Franta needed to speed up his action.

In all their haste this morning, coupled with taking time to write the letter to his parents, Franta hadn't finished his oatmeal and bread and was feeling a bit famished. He wasn't sure if the train was swaying or just what was happening. His head was thumping, as he kept shifting his feet to gain a better footing. He grew hotter and hotter. It was probably just from the heat radiating from the firebox. This went on for a time when at last Peter walked up behind him, reaching his hands under Franta's armpits to back him away from the fire, grabbing the shovel, and sitting his cousin down on a bench nearby.

"Hey, hey, over here," Peter yelled above the roar as he shoveled feverishly to keep the pressure up.

The fireman came over at last. Seeing Franta slumped over on the bench, he ran to get some water. Sitting him up, he shook his shoulders to bring him around.

"Here, take some water. You're dehydrated," he said.

Peter kept on shoveling until the fireman finished tending to Franta.

"That was a close call, man."

They let him rest a while as someone handed him a sandwich. While getting so caught up in his work, he hadn't taken time to care for himself.

"You would have been a fried egg if you had fallen into that fire," Peter said.

"Ya," is all Franta said in reply.

Thirteen

Unless you knew your way around Chicago, one wouldn't have known where they were. Much to the family's amazement when they stepped onto the platform, a young man and woman were standing there with a sign in their hand that read: THOMAS JELINEK FAMILY.

How did they know where and when to pick us up? Franta wondered. What he did not know is that Thomas had called his cousin, Adolph, from the Boarding House unbeknownst to anyone in the family. Adolph then came to the train depot to check on arrivals. He had a fairly good idea of how long it would take since the trains ran pretty much on schedule. The men shook hands; the women hugged.

With the steamer trunk unloaded and their greetings behind them, they loaded the wagon to travel to their temporary stop off. The children chortled as the wagon bumped along the cobblestone street that bordered Lake Michigan.

"Look, *voda*," Albert shouted when he saw the water.

One could almost feel the combined sense of relief that they had made it this far. Even though they still had memories of the stench of vomit and urine from on board their vessel, they would soon be able to put that behind them.

Cousin Adolph gave their visitors an overview of what they were seeing. "Pilsen is serving as a port of entry for folks like you coming in," he said. "Over there is the Bohemia Club, for those who have money to go there. We are now passing the Sokal Hall and up the street is the Czech National Cemetery." Adolph went on to tell them about the Svobodna Obec they founded 17 years ago for the Bohemian Freethinkers. About 80 percent of the Bohemians coming over wanted to escape the oppression of the Habsburg Empire, also leaving behind the Catholic Religion. The Obec was founded for secular baptisms, marriages, and social gatherings. Seven years later, in 1877, they formed a fraternal organization for helping one another if they were out of work or needed help when they got sick. They were nearing Pulaski Road and Foster

Avenues and would soon be out of Pilsen and into Praha where their cousins were living

Thomas listened as Adolph told of the advancements the Bohemians were making on the west side of Chicago. "*Sestra* Rose and I plan to travel westward as well. We want to farm near the town of Wahoo. First we have some business to take care of here before we meet up with you in Nebraska."

Franta and Peter listened intently as Adolph related their experiences since they came across. It appeared to truly be a "land of opportunity" as was evident from what these two cousins had been able to accomplish in the few years they had been here.

"Rose has pork dinner waiting after you wash up and arrange your belongings," Adolph said. "Get a good night's rest before I take you back to catch your train to Omaha."

They hadn't eaten a solid meal since the family had started their arduous journey from their native Bohemia. Rose had prepared roast pork, *knedlicky* and *Kyselé zelí* (dumplings and sauerkraut) and fresh rye bread. For dessert they had something entirely new to them, American apple pie made from the apples that fell from a tree in the neighboring park area where the children played.

"When Adolph and I get to Wahoo, Nebraska, we both plan to marry someone we meet there and have families. If there is a son, he will be named Adolph and if there is a daughter her name shall be Rose after me," Rose said.

Heads reeled from all the information their cousin told them. Franta was still feeling the effects of the heat exhaustion he had suffered earlier. While wishing he could go out and explore the new territory around their house, he decided it would be best to drink lots of water, eat a good supper and get a good night's sleep.

After dinner, Adolph suggested they walk over to the Sokal Hall and listen to the band playing that evening.

"Every Czech is a musician," Adolph said. "Many of our countryman brought along their instruments, so they gather on Saturday night for music and polka dancing. It's entertaining and lots of fun."

Energized by the evening repast, Franta and Peter could scarcely wait to have a diversion from the hum drum they had experienced from the trip over the sea as well as their recent rail trip from New York City. They were ready for some levity – the entire family was as well.

"Just listen to the oom-pa-pa of that tuba," Adolph said smiling brightly. "If only I could play that well."

"If I could play a tuba, I'd play it even better than that," Franta said jokingly.

Thomas and Josepha kicked off their shoes and twirled around the floor. *It is joyous to see that Thomas has a fun side to his nature,* Franta thought.

The children joined hands and jumped around the floor. Everyone was having a good time. The clock struck midnight.

"We must be getting back to your house," Thomas said to Adolph. "You have shown us what life in America is like."

Franta tossed and turned that night. Perhaps it was realizing that his journey would soon take him to his ultimate destination. He fumbled in his pants pocket to find the folded paper he had been carrying that read, *Farm Workers Needed – Brainard, Nebraska.* Beneath the heading it said *contact The Union Pacific Railroad.* He liked how he felt here in Chicagoland. Should he stay here and work for someone where there was access to everything he would ever need? He might find a wife here eventually, one that was Bohemian and would cook the same foods his mother had cooked back home. He knew he wanted a family: sons to help farm and who would play musical instruments and form a band and daughters to be a help to his wife. He carefully folded the paper back up and put it into the pocket of the pants on the floor next to him. If he stayed here, he would never have land like he had dreamed of when he walked back and forth to the mines at Kladno. His eyes finally grew weary and he decided he would sleep on it. Things always seemed easier by daylight.

Cousin Rose was busy stirring in the kitchen when he and his relatives gathered. There was nothing like the aroma of bacon frying to bring people to the table. Her large, blue coffee pot simmered on the stove as she whipped up a bowlful of eggs to scramble. Aunt Josepha grabbed an apron from the hook behind the kitchen door as she brought dishes out of the cupboard to set the table.

"You can pour some apple juice, Rosalia," Rose said to her cousin. "There was a bumper crop of apples this year that I still need to put up."

"You're quiet this morning. Didn't you sleep well?" quizzed Peter to his cousin.

"I slept fine. I need to get food into my stomach and I'll be ready to hit the rails again." Franta said. Something inside told him he must continue on toward his dream even though staying in Chicagoland was tempting.

The women cleaned up after breakfast and the men helped Adolph get some of the outside chores done before they took off for the depot. They needed to be there by 11:00 a.m.

The family bid Adolph and Rose a fond farewell as they thanked them for putting them up for the night and taking them back to the railroad station.

Franta checked in with the conductor as to where he would find the fireman to begin his stoking duties to Omaha. He had decided one thing for certain. When he got to Nebraska, he did not want to ever shovel coal again and especially not to earn a living.

Fourteen

The little he could see from his firebox, Franta's eyes looked out over flat land as far as his eyes could see. Miles and miles of land. He heard the passengers in the background, as they careened their necks out the window talking about the corn that was raised on this ground. The stoking wasn't nearly as strenuous as it had been earlier in the hilly regions, but still, he had to keep up a steady pace of pouring the coal into the giant black monster of an engine.

He caught a glimpse of the Illinois River, then later the Mississippi River. Some people were chattering about how this was the land that President Abraham Lincoln had come from. They had heard stories about the famous man who was shot while attending a play at Ford's Theatre. There was so much for him to learn about this new land.

He could see acres of fertile farm ground that was ripe for the harvest of corn. The stalks were as tall as a grown man with three ears to a stalk as farmers drove in between the rows with their wagons pulled by a team of horses. The huskers walked along side, shucking corn and throwing it into a wagon with sideboards. He could only dream now about how one day soon, he too would have his own corn to harvest.

Their train trip from Chicago took them almost due west on the Illinois Central until they reached Rock Island, Illinois, where the train then changed the name to the Rock Island Railroad. He couldn't begin to understand why they named them differently and yet stayed on the same train.

"Better go take time to eat lunch with your family," the fireman said to him.

Franta welcomed the break and remembered that he needed to drink plenty of water. His back ached from leaning over, so stretching and eating was welcome. Together, with Peter, they peered out the window at the new land that almost took their breath away. *It's getting closer and soon I'll be on my own.* A burst of fear gripped him at the thought of being alone for the very first time in his life. The train ride was to take eight hours and they were about six hours into it. That would put them into Omaha about seven o'clock that night. It was gut wrenching to think he and Peter wouldn't be seeing one another for a long time. He couldn't think of that now. He had work to do as he walked over to his post near the firebox.

The sun glowed like a giant ball of fire over the horizon as they crossed the Missouri River. Another hour or so to go and they would be in Omaha, Nebraska. He wondered what his uncle had planned for the night. Omaha is where Franta will part ways with Peter and his family who will go on to Lincoln and from there they plan to go to Saline County to homestead.

He guessed he would stretch out on one of the benches in the depot to be ready to head out on the Union Pacific Railroad from Omaha to Brainard, only an hour and a half away. It was all becoming a reality.

The locomotive lumbered its way on the last leg of Franta's journey to his final destination. Above the sound of his shovel scraping the coal bin, he listened as the conductor announced the towns ahead.

"Elkorn, Mead, Wahoo, Weston, Valparaiso, Brainard."

Franta listened carefully to the sounds of the town names since his understanding of English was limited. He looked forward to being in a community where most of the people spoke his native Bohemian tongue. Primary school taught him some English words, but only the bare necessities. He longed for a real conversation again now that his cousin was no longer with him.

The changing colors were his calendar as the green faded from the leaves and they turned a brilliant golden. He counted the days in his mind figuring it must be nearing the end of September. He would have enough time to find a job as a farm worker and secure a place to live. He reminded himself every day to take it one day at a time.

On the downward slopes, he could ease up on the stoking. He took out the folded advertisement from his pocket and looked at it once again hoping some mysterious message would appear telling him what to do.

"Mead," the Conductor called out. Then, "Wahoo."

Only two more places to go before we get there, he thought. *At least it will still be daylight which will make it easier for me to get around.*

Fifteen

They rumbled through Weston and Valparaiso just long enough to drop off mail with no other passengers on board. Franta continued with his coal stoking job. He had definitely earned his passage and then some.

"Brainard," the Conductor announced at the top of his voice as if there were many noisy passengers on board.

Franta stowed the shovel on a hook outside of the coal bin. He gathered up his satchel that contained his only earthly possessions, the clothes he purchased from the Salvation Army Used Clothing store in New York City. It had only been a few days ago since he was there sweeping the floor, yet somehow it seemed like weeks ago. He thanked the fireman and the conductor. Just as he stepped onto the platform of the depot, the engineer came over.

"Do you have someplace to spend the night?" the Engineer asked.

Franta understood his words, but with his limited English, he simply shook his head from side to side.

"There's a boarding house on the north side where our crew has stayed a time or two. I'm sure she'd have a room until you get your bearings. Maybe she has some odd jobs she needs to have done in exchange. Tell her Loco Jack sent you."

Franta repeated what he said over and over so he would remember. He walked out onto the platform, looked up and down as far as he could see and there was little there. *What am I going to do next?* He thought. Tipping the grey and white stripped railroad cap he'd been given, he walked down the steps and set out on foot in the general direction that Loco Jack had given him. He walked along the track for a ways and then decided he better move to the west so that he was still in town, such as it was, and continue on. He passed the grain elevator, lumber yard, blacksmith shop, and livery stable. That was pretty much all he saw. He came across the house that had a sign with English words he could not read, but he took a chance going up the steps and to the door.

"*Halo*," Franta said. The lady behind the screen door introduced herself as Zenka. "Loco Jack say maybe I stay here. I do work for you? You let me sleep?" he said.

"I sure do. Come on in. You look mighty tired, son," she said. Zenka showed him his room. She showed him where the outside privy was and where he could take a bath in a long, metal tub. Tomorrow you can wash your clothes in the creek. "I'll heat some water for your bath. But, first, why don't I have you chop some wood for me? There's a black walnut tree over there. You can gather some of them green walnuts, knock off their husks and tonight you can break them open out on the back porch."

Franta's feet drug as he went out back to work. He stacked his chopped wood up carefully where she had told him and then went over to gather walnuts. He had never tasted them back home. By then his water was warm enough to dump into the metal wash tub in the shed out back. It felt good to get the grit, grime and soot off of his body. The bar of lye soap Aunt Josepha gave him would have to last him awhile, so he used it sparingly.

He emerged from his bath, bright and refreshed, feeling like a new person. There wasn't anything as refreshing as water.

"Creek?" he signaled gesturing in hope she knew where he could scrub the clothes he'd worn shoveling coal.

"You can walk east of town two miles and you will find Oak Creek. I have some stew on the stove. Bet you could eat a hot meal with biscuits," she said.

"Yes, Ma'am," he'd learned to say in English.

When Zenka and he had finished eating, Franta went out to the back porch to skin the walnuts. He couldn't believe how oily they made his hands. His mind wondered how that oil could be squeezed out to be used for something. He was always thinking of ways to make things easier. Like the men at the tavern always told him, "Why do things the easy way when the hard way will work?" Then they would laugh. This stayed with him as a good joke.

"I'll cook you breakfast if you want to do some more work for me tomorrow," Zenka said.

Franta nodded his head, "Yes." Then he asked her, "Any Bohemians here?" He was eager to get together with others who had come to work for the railroad or in the fields.

"When you go east to the countryside to find the river, you will find people of your kind in the fields picking corn," she replied.

His anxiety was lessened now that he was bathed, fed and had made a friend who could tell him where things are. He slept well again, just like when he was in Chicagoland with his cousins.

Sixteen

He walked the two miles east of Brainard where he discovered Oak Creek. It was running low, yet there was enough water for him to soak the sooty clothes he wore on the train ride over. He pounded them against the rocks and used the lye soap around the collar of his shirt as well as the socks and under-wear. Franta had watched his mother wash clothes often and sometimes he even hung them up to dry for her. Luckily, it was a warm autumn day so he could stay around until his clothes were dry enough to carry back to the boarding house where he could hang them on the clothesline there. He wondered why Zenka hadn't offered to do this laundry chore for him in exchange for some physical chore.

"Do you come here often?" he heard a voice downstream speaking in his native tongue.

"This is my first time here. I just got into town yesterday," he said to a young girl, pleased that he could converse fluently with someone once again since being with his relatives.

She looked like she was about ten years old. He wondered why she was roaming around alone out in the country.

"My parents are picking corn in the field over there. They don't make me do it since I have brothers that can help them, but I wanted to come along anyway because I didn't want to stay behind by myself."

"Who do they work for?" Franta asked.

"I can't exactly remember the name of the land owner, but they will be able to tell you."

As soon as Franta got his laundry done and hung on the trees to dry some, he asked the girl if she would lead him to where her parents were working. She obliged, but first she wanted to know.

"What's your name?"

"Franta."

"That's my father's name too, but here in America everyone calls him Frank. You might want to call yourself Frank too," the girl said.

"What do you go by?" Franta asked.

"Anezka," she replied. "I'm named after my aunt back in Moravia.

They walked a ways away from the creek and over to the field where her family was picking. The corn stalks were dry and crunched beneath their feet.

"*Maminka, Táta* , look who I found. Maybe he can help you get this field done before night."

Franta introduced himself and told the father that he just got into Brainard and where he was staying. "Anezka says you might need some help."

It seemed good to talk to a fellow countryman. "My name is Frank also, and this is my wife, Milada. Over there are my two sons, Emil and Adolph. How old are you, son?"

"I just turned 12, but *Táta* showed me how to work. People say I look old for my age."

"Where are your parents, Frank?"

"They are still in Bohemia. I came over with my aunt and uncle, but they wanted to settle in Saline County, so we split apart in Omaha. I had a flyer about working and getting land by Brainard," Frank told him.

"You came all the way over without your parents at the age of twelve. You are a brave young man. Were things that bad for you over there?"

"I was working in a coal mine with my father and hated the work. It was so dirty. Besides, I want to own my own land and be a farmer. Over there that wasn't possible."

"I want to have my own place too. Maybe we can all be neighbors one day."

"Who should I talk to about work?" he asked his new friend, Frank.

"His name is Anton Houbovy, Sr. He and his wife live on the edge of town. I'm sure if you ask, someone can tell you how to find them."

Franta finished helping his new friends pick corn and then went back over to the creek to pick up his clothes. He was enthused to have met the family who were helpful in giving him useful information. Tomorrow he would set out to find the landowner and see about working for hire.

"Well, you're back. I began to wonder about you," Zenka said as Franta hung his wet clothing on her line to finish drying. "I made some ham and beans for us to eat. Are you hungry?"

Franta ate like he had a hollow leg. "I'll pay you back for this good food after I start earning some money," he told her.

"Don't you worry about that. There's always plenty for you to do around here."

milk them too. The land was wide open, and the grass grew tall so the cows would have plenty to eat.

Mr. Houbovy said, "Those cows will just keep eating and eating until they are in someone else's property unless there's someone to watch them. I'll pay you 50 cents a day with room and board."

They had a herd of nine milk cows and a bull. The job didn't sound very difficult to him, but he had to learn the ways of the bovines. He received instructions from the owner on which was the lead cow that the herd followed. These animals were called Holsteins, whose hide was spotted black and white. They were known to be good for producing milk. Mr. Houbovy cautioned Frank not to let the cows graze on the neighbor's property. He went out with him the first day to show him what hog grass looked like and not to let them eat any because it tainted the milk. The Houbovys had a corral that penned the herd overnight, and then they needed to be herded out to the pasture grass. There were no fences to be seen anywhere. Back in Bohemia there were stone fences everywhere which made this land look barren.

"Here, you'll need this," Mr. Houbovy said as he handed Frank a water skin to take along with him as well as a tin bucket that had some food in it for his noon meal. The water skin, made from a cow's bladder and covered with canvas, kept the well water cool naturally throughout the day. Young Frank's mind marveled at what he was learning so quickly about farming. "Bring the herd in when you see the sun dipping toward the horizon," he instructed him. Frank was somewhat leery about what he would do if something came along to spook them.

"What should I do if I can't get them to go where I want?" he asked.

"You get acquainted with Bossy, the lead cow, and she will follow you. Always look her in the eyes and rub her hind quarter to get her to trust you."

Frank set out to steer the Holstein herd out to the pasture. He made sure he had his pocket knife and harmonica to pass his time away. He wondered how it would be out there all alone and if there were any wild dogs or wolves roaming around. He would have to find a herder's crook.

Late that afternoon, Frank steered the herd back to the owner's place. He saw as the cows' utters were beginning to swell that they would soon needed to be milked. Mrs. Houbovy handed Frank the galvanized bucket and a three-legged milk stool their son had used when he was still with them. She offered no explanation of what had happened to him and Frank was not about to bring it up.

"Since you've never milked before, let me give you some instructions," she told him.

They waited until the herd settled down from their walk from the grazing. Then the missus took the lead cow as hers to be milked with Frank looking over her shoulder.

"First, we wash off the utter with this clean cloth in case they've walked through anything that would contaminate the milk. Also, it signals the cow to begin undulating."

She handed him the cloth and took hold of her first two teats. As she sat on the stool with the bucket in between her knees, she began to squeeze the teats alternately. Within a few seconds, the milk gave a sound against the bucket. When the first two teats felt almost empty, she went to the back two and repeated the process. After they were nearly empty, she went back to the first two and began to use a stripping motion to empty out the utter.

"Now, one thing you always have to watch out for is that the cow doesn't kick. Ours are not noted to be kickers, but sometimes when it gets hot out, they go after flies. So always be ready to grab her leg or get out of the way," Sylvia added.

"Now, you take your stool and bucket and let's see if you've got the hang of it," she said.

Frank was a natural for it. He was a quick learner, and as he drew the first squirts of milk, he was thrilled. He had never thought about milking cows before. Gathered around were the farm's cats, Mama and her youngsters, always hoping the milker would shoot some milk their way. Frank knew he wouldn't win any milking contests with his speed but gave himself some credit realizing, like with anything else, it would take time to get the job done quickly. Sylvia and Frank finished off the milking chores within the hour and headed back toward the house where she would get their evening meal on the table.

"Thank you, Ma'am, for the good meal. It makes me think of *Maminka*. She fed me good."

As they learned a little more about Frank and his family back in Bohemia, Frank asked Sylvia if she had a paper and a pencil so he could send his parents a letter.

"Such a thoughtful young man," she said to her husband when they retired that night. "You did well by hiring him to help us out."

The days were beginning to cast long shadows reminding Frank that winter would be upon them in a few weeks. He wondered how the cows would get their feed when snow covered the prairie. Anton was quick to fill him in.

"You see that stack of hay over there," Anton said. "When you're no longer herding, you will pitch hay to the cows in the corral. As soon as the lumber gets here, we'll set out to build a barn for our herd," he told him.

Frank looked around the room they had given him upstairs. It was really more of an attic than an upstairs, but he couldn't complain. For the things that hung on the wall, he could tell it had been their son's room. Maybe, one day they would tell him what happened to him. Feeling content after writing to his family back in Europe, Frank fell exhausted on the bed to sleep soundly and ready to tackle whatever the couple had in store for him the next day.

Eighteen

The young farmer headed out the door with his water skin, his lunch bucket, pocket knife, and harmonica. Sylvia gave him a tattered blanket he could use on the ground as he sat watching the herd. This was the first time he'd had to try to eke out some of the old tunes he remembered from the old country. They were mostly tavern songs, polkas, and such. He would work on his favorite, *Tá Naše Písnička Česká* that speaks of beautiful songs from Bohemia. Thinking of the song tugged at his heart as his thoughts went back to his mother and father. *Maybe they will come join me here one day. If only they knew it is so beautiful here too.*

As he drew in breaths on the instrument and blew into it, the cows all looked around in total wonder. He had to laugh out loud as he thought about his first audience. This was something he could tell his children someday. Frank loved music. He also liked to dance. As he sat on the ragged old blanket under a bright blue autumn sky, he worked and worked at the melody until something recognizable came through. *When I get this to where it sounds right, I'll play for Anton and Sylvia after supper some night, but not until I'm happy with it.*

Frank was so glad he had picked this spot in Nebraska in which to settle. There were mostly his own kind here who all had the same aim in life: to succeed and live happily. He didn't mind the monotonous work since he didn't really have anything to spend his money on. The Houbovys gave him a roof over his head and meals. They treated him well and talked like they appreciated the job he was doing for them.

Every day they hoped the lumber and nails would come for the barn. Eagerly he awaited learning something new so one day he could build his own house and barn. The cows would be happy to have a place out of the snow everyone said was coming this winter.

The autumn air had a chill to it, and the leaves from the cottonwood trees along Oak Creek lined the banks of the stream. Frank continued to practice his music on the harmonica. It almost seemed to him the cows were beginning to enjoy it. At first, as they looked at him big-eyed, then lifting their heads upwards letting out a moo or two, they settled into noshing on the lush prairie grass.

As he bent and twisted, working the harp with his mouth and tongue, he quickly learned that he could create various sounds. It reminded him of the button accordions played in the taverns he frequented with his father on Sunday afternoons back in Kladno. Intently working to bring forth a tune, he was suddenly jarred out of his musical interlude when he felt a sudden jolt on his shoulder. Standing up and turning around, he was face to face with a tall painted face. *Jezis, Maria, an Indian. What do I do now?*

The man, with reddish skin, pointed fiercely to the mouth harp. Frank couldn't tell what exactly he was getting at. Frank put the harmonica to his lips and made a sound. The Indian grinned with all his tobacco stained teeth showing. He pointed to the mouth then back to himself. Frank stood his ground waiting for the intruder to make his move. He didn't have a chance to reach into his pocket for his knife, and even if he had, it didn't seem that the man meant any harm or he would have done it earlier when he snuck up behind him.

"*Muzika*", Frank said to him.

The man, dressed in buckskins and wearing strands of beads, motioned to Frank and back to himself. The actions signified to him that the man wanted the harmonica. *I don't want to give it up, but yet, he is much bigger than I am so I wouldn't stand a chance taking him on.*

Frank continued to just stand there.

The Indians in the area were known to be of the Sioux Tribe. There were few around and stories were such that the group was peaceful.

"Me want," the man said pointing to the instrument.

Just as I'm learning to play it, I don't want to give it up, but what else can I do?

The Indian reached to take off a strand of brightly colored beads. He seemed willing to bargain. He held the beads out in front of himself with his right hand, coming ever so close to Frank and with the other hand, he gestured for the shiny mouth harp trimmed in red. Frank had no choice but to hand it to him as the two exchanged their possessions. The Sioux would go back to his camp with the harmonica and Frank would go home with a string of beads. Meanwhile the herd was steadily moving farther and farther away from the spot.

Frank knew his first responsibility was to keep the cows out of the weeds, so he turned, picked up his blanket, flask, and lunch and headed toward the cattle. As he looked back, the visitor slipped away as swiftly and quietly as he had arrived.

Nineteen

After putting the cattle securely into the corral, Frank noticed the lumber had arrived, stacked for easy access to building. *I gave up my harmonica for a string of beads and even though my heart is heavy, there is new hope with the material here. We'll be building soon.*

Pausing at the water pump to draw a bucket of fresh water to carry in with him, Frank was eager to tell Anton and Sylvia what had happened to him on the prairie. First though, the herd needed to be milked. Reaching for a clean bucket, Frank found comfort with his head in the flank of Bossy, and as he felt her energy pulsate through his body, he was grateful that the Indian was not hostile. He had his life and that was what mattered.

When milking chores were done, Frank lumbered up the porch and into the kitchen. Sylvia said, "What's with the long face?"

Frank didn't realize he was wearing his feelings on his face. He said, "I'll tell you all about it over supper."

The three filled their plates. Sylvia made chicken and dumplings which pleased the pallet. When most of his food was eaten, Frank began to relate his tale of the Sioux and the loss of his harmonica. Reaching into his overalls, he pulled out the strand of beads the Indian had traded with no conscious choice. Anton laughed a bit. Frank didn't find much humor in it. Sylvia noticed Frank's disappointment and quickly said, "You can always get another one."

"Did you see the wood stacked up near the corral?" Anton asked. "We can start as soon as I get some of the neighbors together. You can take time off from herding to help with the barn raising. We'll corral the cows while you are working on the barn with us. When it's done, we'll have a celebration." The anticipation of having something new and interesting to do helped take his mind off of his loss. He figured he'd need to watch closely and even make some sketches as it was going along so by the time he could build one, he wouldn't forgot how it was done.

"I'm calling it a night," Frank said as his feet moved up the creaking stairs up to his room.

By noon the next day, four of their neighbors were on the farmstead with their hammers and saws. It would be a good day. He heard Anton say that if there was money left after the barn was up, they could start on putting up some fence. Everyone was talking about the fairly new barbed wire that could be strung between fence posts. If they could fence in the pasture, Frank could spend his time with the cultivating and planting. Things were looking up.

The men worked at a feverish pace to get the barn raised before weather set in. It was common for this part of the country to experience an early snowfall, so they wanted to get it done ahead of any such storms.

As was the custom, the woman baked pies and their Bohemian pastries, the *kolaches*, along with the traditional sandwiches that consisted of a slice of homemade white bread cut at an angle, covered with a slice of ham, topped with potato salad and a slice of dill pickle. There was plenty of coffee brewed in the blue porcelain coffee pot atop the stove.

As they filed past the spread laid out on a table in the yard, Frank thought back to the pastries his mother used to make. They were a yeast dough, filled with a sweet poppy seed filling that he didn't know exactly what was in it. He remembered that she deep fried them. She then sprinkled powdered sugar on top. He remembered how they melted in his mouth. They were called *buchty* in Bohemian.

"Sylvia, do you ever make *buchty*, or does anyone else around here make them?" he asked.

"I think that is more of a Moravian dish. I learned the ways of my mother and she wasn't from Moravia," she replied.

How he longed for the taste of these. As long as he let his mind go there, he wondered about his cousin. *I'm wondering what he's doing and if he misses me as much as I miss him. One day we may be able to reunite once more,* he thought.

The stair steps creaked once more as Frank climbed up to his room after their long day of work. From the way it looked, the men would have it done in two more days. He looked forward to the extra food. Even at his young age, he stood 5 feet 10 inches tall and had a robust body. He would ask Anton if he would teach him how to shave with his straight edge shaver. He used to watch his father shave, but didn't pay close enough attention so as not to cut his neck or ear. It looked complicated. Sylvia told him once that when he was ready she could trim his reddish blonde hair. He'd wait until the work was behind them and they would be settling in for fall.

Twenty

The barn was up and the cattle were happy to be in out of the cold. It was good to be able to milk inside. Anton and Frank prepared wood for the coming winter. They cut up some of the scraps from the barn to use as kindling. They also had a cob pile from the corn Anton had shelled earlier. Cobs produced a nice warm fire. Some of the farmers used cow chips, but Sylvia wouldn't have them in her kitchen. They used the wagon and horses to bring wood up from along Oak Creek where trees had fallen down. Anton and his son had brought up wood last fall so it was good and dry for cutting to be used this winter. The new wood they hauled up would be left to dry to be cut up again next fall.

Frank helped saw the wood into pieces that he then split with an axe. His arms ached at night, yet he was proud when he checked his arms to see the muscles he was developing from the upper arm labor.

For some odd reason, he thought about the Indian and wondered if the native was able to produce his people's brand of music. He thought, too, about Uncle Thomas and Aunt Josepha and the cousins. *Even though Uncle was upset that I had come along, he must be over it by now.* His memories lulled him to sleep as he thought about the next day of making wood.

They woke to a mild mist the next morning. Anton told Frank he could take the day to do whatever he liked. Frank had been wanting to walk up town, and the mist wasn't coming down hard enough to stop him from doing that. He walked by the blacksmith shop noting the red hot forge and the "smithie" pounding away at his latest project. Eager to see where the Logan store and post office were, Frank continued on his way. He passed the Brainard State Bank, owned by A.K. Smith that would be opening in just about two weeks. They had heard the owner was from way east from the state of Vermont. The Holy Trinity Catholic Church would be built soon along with the one-room school. He walked to the edge of town where he saw the familiar depot to the Omaha & Republican Valley Railroad Company on which he had come to town.

The village also had the Brown Cemetery and soon the Catholic Cemetery was to open.

It seemed like so much had taken place in such a short time, it made his head swim. He reached the post office where several rows of 11 x 6 x ¼ inch ornate metal boxes with combination locks on the fronts lined the wall so mail would be safe. There was a general delivery box where those who didn't rent a private box could ask the post master to sift through to find their mail. Frank was eager to get a reply from his mother to the letter he had sent when he first arrived in town. He often thought it may have gotten lost, but none the less, he never gave up hope of hearing from her.

He took his time browsing through the store, looking especially for one item.

"You don't happen to have a harmonica?" he asked the lady behind the counter.

"We don't just yet, but they say the Sears and Roebuck Catalog sells them by mail order. If you decide you want one, let me know and I can order it for you."

Frank was pleased to get that information even though he wasn't prepared to order one just yet. He forever kept in mind the money he needed to save in order to purchase the land he wanted when he turned 18.

As he walked back home, he heard the panting of a dog behind him. He reached down to pet the black and white tail-wagger walking beside him now.

"You better get along home now," Frank commanded.

But the pooch just looked up at him with deep dark eyes that seemed to say, "Take me home and feed me."

Frank wasn't sure what he should do about the mutt, so he just let him come along. He would ask Sylvia and Anton what they thought.

Upon reaching the back door, Anton greeted him.

"What do you have here?" he asked.

"I can't seem to shake him. I told him to go home, but he won't listen," Frank replied.

"I've got some scraps we can feed him. We'll leave him out here on the porch and see if he leaves after he's eaten."

Frank secretly hoped the dog would stay. He could use him for help with herding and for companionship. The mist continued as Frank went inside to get dry and warm up. Soon his uninvited guest was forgotten. That evening after supper, Anton reached atop the shelf in the parlor for a deck of cards.

"The three of us can play a game of cards," Anton said. Since they had an uneven number they couldn't play *Taroky*, so they dealt up a game of *Prsi* which is played like the American game of Crazy Eights. Sylvia popped some popcorn they had grown in their large garden out back. Filling the bowl, she tucked away the iron skillet to be used for breakfast in the morning. The three of them played cards well past ten o'clock. Frank told the couple about his day browsing around downtown.

"They could use a few more businesses, especially someplace to buy clothes," he said.

He enjoyed listening to the rain as it came down on the roof of his upstairs bedroom. He thought about what he'd get Anton and Sylvia for Christmas. They had been so good to him; he needed to figure out something to make since he was saving every Friday's pay toward the farm he dreamed about every day. *I'm too sleepy to worry about that tonight. Something will come to me in the coming days.*

"Oh, you're still here," Frank said to the black and white stray as he walked out the door the next morning. "I will call you *Kamos* and we'll be buddies."

Twenty One

A chill in the air signaled the coming of fall and winter. Frank didn't know for sure what to expect of the coming winter weather except for what others had told him. Winds from the north could be frigid they told him. When the ground froze, the herding would be over. They would feed the cattle from prairie hay that they had stored in the hay mow of the new barn. The cows were slowing down on milk production and soon some would go dry. This dairy farming was all new to him, yet he liked learning about things that he would one day do when he had a farm of his own.

Sylvia skimmed the cream from the top of the milk that they kept in the root cellar. Temperatures there were cool where milk would last longer. The temperature remained constant throughout summer and winter at around 38 to 40 degrees. She made quite a bit of cheese. Frank liked the cottage cheese that they put caraway seeds into. She called it *syr*, the same as they did in Bohemia.

The root cellar was intriguing to Frank. Anton and his son dug out a patch of ground about 6 x 6 x 10 feet. They didn't need to worry about tree roots since there were few trees except for those along Oak Creek. They decided to put it to the back of the house where it was easier access from the back door to the kitchen. Anton remembered it took them some time picking and digging as they slanted the sides so the walls wouldn't fall in. Frank wished he had been around to watch how they had done it. Steps were built going down and a door placed on top to keep it closed and dark. The cellar dome had a vent to keep the gasses from the fruits and vegetables circulating. By the time he had arrived, there were shelves where Sylvia and Anton stored potatoes, carrots, onions, and turnips as well as apples they bought in David City from the few growers there. Sylvia stored pork in a large stone crock covered with lard from the hog they butchered. She also stored Mason jars of canned tomatoes, meat, corn, wild plum jam, and just about anything that wouldn't keep over the winter. The invention of the glass jar around 1858 was a blessing to farmers.

There were so many things Frank had taken for granted until now that he would have to know how to survive on his own eventually. With all he had crammed into his head so far, there was still one nagging question. It would satisfy his curiosity if the couple would talk about why their son left them. What surprised him was that none of the neighbors ever mentioned it either. There was something strange about this.

"Would you like to come with me to a farm sale on Saturday?" Anton asked Frank. "The couple on the far section near Abie are pulling up stakes. They say they've had enough. We might be able to pick up some things real cheap. Sylvia, you come along too."

Frank looked forward to the new adventure. He didn't know what to expect, but was always eager for a new experience. He heard them say it would take place even if it rained or snowed.

The three of them bundled up and climbed onto the hay wagon laden with provisions of water, food, and extra blankets in case the weather turned cold before they got back home. Frank learned to hitch the team to the wagon a few weeks earlier during corn picking time.

"Where does a person get the harnesses for the team and where did this team come from?" he asked Anton.

"Same way. When farmers decide this life is too much work for them, they hold a farm sale. This way of life will all be worth it once we get everything the way we want it. But, it takes time."

Frank was taken aback when he saw all the people standing around visiting with one another while others looked at pieces of equipment they might be interested in bidding on. The farmer pulled the cord on the large dinner bell as the auctioneer took his place up on a wooden crate where everyone could see him. They had a desk close by where another man sat with a long black notebook ready to record each sale.

"Now, Frank, keep your hands and arms down and don't touch your face because those are signals you are bidding on an item. Watch how it works and you'll get the idea."

Anton had his eye on the hand scythe that he planned to bid on so that they would have another one in order for Frank to help cut the hay and harvest the wheat. Frank tucked his hands into his overalls to keep them out of sight and watched as the bidding went on. Not everyone paid attention to the auction. Some were off in the distance visiting, others still looking at items displayed.

Frank looked around as well, hoping to find something he could afford that he could get Anton and Sylvia for Christmas. They had been so kind to him and helpful as well as giving him a job and a roof over his head.

He smelled the coffee brewing over an open fire in a blue and white speckled coffee pot. "Come and have a cup," the man said to Frank. "I don't think I know you."

"I've only been over here a few months," Frank told him.

"Is your family here? Where do you live?" he asked.

"They're still in the old country. I came alone."

Frank was somewhat cautious talking about himself and how he came, for fear that someone there might be working for the government and find out that he didn't have any papers. He didn't want to be sent back. Not after he'd made his way this far.

The scythe came up for bid and luckily there wasn't too much interest in it, so Anton got it fairly cheap. Frank kept wondering if the dinner bell would be sold. He thought that would be a nice gift for his surrogate parents. When the sale was coming to a close, they hadn't offered the bell for auction. Frank waited until just before they were about to leave and went up to the farmer and made him an offer of 50 cents. Not only did it serve a useful purpose for gathering everyone for meals, but it looked nice and it reminded him of bells that pealed back home. Frank, delighted with his purchase, buried it under some burlap bags in the back of the wagon, while Anton was talking to another farmer.

It had been a good day. The weather held; Anton got his scythe, and Frank was able to see what a farm sale was all about. They bid the people still left farewell and headed for home with their new purchases.

Twenty Two

There was no Catholic Church in Brainard at this time, yet a small parish was growing in Center a few miles to the west. While many of the menfolk were Free Thinkers who came to America, many of their womenfolk still clung to the ideals they grew up with. Anton realized that Sylvia yearned to celebrate Mass over the Christmas holiday, so he promised her that if the weather was suitable, he would take her by wagon to Mass.

There were no formal roads yet, only paths the farmers took to get supplies such as seed, lumber, and such. Anton would need to take lanterns along to light their way. "I'd like you to come with us, Frank. You can hold one of the lanterns while I handle the reins," Anton told Frank a few days before Christmas. The service will be at five o'clock instead of the traditional midnight mass that was held in the old country. This was to help farmers to make the trip before it got real late.

"Whatever helps," Frank replied. He thought he'd attend Mass himself, curious as to how it might differ here from his homeland.

They had counted on some moonlight, but the night was black as coal as they made their way home around seven. The ride by wagon would take about an hour. Sylvia baked the traditional *houska* that they would have when they got home along with coffee and cream. Frank looked forward to the yeast bread that was chock-full with nuts, and raisins braided in it. His heart was heavy as he thought of his mother whose delicious meals and pastries he had enjoyed along with all the festivities she provided. Here, there was no Christmas tree, no candles, or music. It was different, but someday, he'd make sure it was the same again as it was in his old country.

After they ate the meal Sylvia had prepared ahead consisting of breaded white fish along with her *houska*, Anton carried out two items from the upstairs bedroom.

"I have a gift for you, my dear Sylvia," he said handing her the box that was wrapped in a damask handkerchief. "I know you have been admiring this for some time at the General Store."

Tears streamed from Sylvia's face as she gazed at the multi colored brooch that glistened in the light of the kerosene lamplight. "Can we afford this?" she asked her husband.

"I can't afford not to give this to you, my *milá*. You work so hard and do without so much to help us build our farm," Anton told his wife.

Frank felt a bit uncomfortable witnessing this tender moment between them. He had not heard his father talk this way to his mother, so it made him feel uneasy.

Next, Anton handed Frank a small package wrapped in newsprint. Frank was taken aback as he had not expected a Christmas present. Anton and Sylvia's eyes were upon him as he untied the twine. His heart dropped to his feet as he gazed on a shiny, red trimmed harmonica. Unable to speak, he put the mouth harp to his lips and slid it back and forth, trying to remember the melodies he had played on the one the red skinned visitor had traded his beads for earlier in the year.

Frank stood up and began to stomp his feet as he drew air in and out, eking out the melody of *Tá Naše Písnička Česká*. The couple clapped their hands as Kamos began to howl and the cat, Kočka, whose eyes grew large, turned tail and flew out of the room.

"That's the stuff. You haven't lost it after all these months," Anton chided.

Suddenly, Frank stopped. He grabbed his coat from the hook near the back door and disappeared outdoors. He had hidden the dinner bell in the barn beneath the hay. Shaking off the stray strands, he came back in and presented the couple with the gift he had been hiding since they went to the farm sale.

"What a thoughtful gift, Frank!" Sylvia can ring the bell at mealtime and we can make it toll at midnight.

Frank thought of how fortunate he was to have found such a kind and thoughtful couple to work for who treated him as if he was their own kin.

They bid one another a Merry Christmas and retired after a memorable night.

Twenty Three

The New Year came unheralded. Only four months had passed in Frank's new land, yet it seemed like he had been here much longer. So much had taken place in his life. After stowing away on the steamship that August day and journeying across the sea with his cousin, he had been so busy he had scarcely had time to miss him, but with the long wintery nights and not as much work to do, there was more time to think. He often thought of how his aunt, uncle, and cousins were faring. He wondered if they had found good people to help them get settled as he had with the Houbovys. There was only one of him, whereas Uncle Thomas had a clan to look after. Perhaps, one day their paths would meet again in a few years.

As Frank lay on the straw mattress covered with a muslin sheet and feather bed, he was able to keep warm in that upstairs bedroom, once belonging to their son. He remembered how the good people in New York helped him at the Inn and especially at the Good Will store – giving him a chance to work to earn much needed clothing. Would his mother be worrying about whether he had enough clothes, and if he was keeping warm enough? His eye felt moist, so he quickly thought about the coal he shoveled on his way to Chicago and how he almost decided to stay there. He could be working in a store there in Little Prague and eating his cousin's good food. Guilt swept over him as he thought about the good food Sylvia made for Anton and him. He had made the right decision to come westward to find a place like Brainard where the land was lush and fertile and where he would be able to realize his dream of having his own ground to farm.

"Did you hear what happened at the General Store?" Anton asked that next afternoon. "A Gypsy wagon came into town yesterday with its canvas top and bobbles hanging down from the sides. While the rest of their party stayed outside, the leader came into the store wearing his white ruffled shirt and red sash with a red and black printed bandana on his head."

"The Gypsy man came in demanding some food stuffs, but soon turned tail and left when Mr. Logan came up with a large knife from behind the counter," Anton said.

"I was warned about Gypsies coming through and robbing stores, so I was ready for him," the storekeeper continued.

"Was anyone else in the store?" Frank asked.

"No one else was there to help out in case the leader decided to get pushy," Anton told them.

That was enough excitement to last them several days to have something new to talk about. When the Gypsy incident subsided, Frank came in for supper with an unbelievable story. He told of what happened to Mrs. Vanek, living near Prague, a few miles north and east of Brainard. She used her clay outdoor oven each time she baked bread for the family. The aroma of the bread drifted throughout the surrounding area and could be smelled for several miles around. On this particular day, Mrs. Vanek was bending over with her long handled bread peel in her hand. As she scraped up the round loaf of bread from the oven, she turned to set it on a nearby flat stone for the bread to cool just as she had many times before.

"Eek," she shrieked as behind her stood a tall Sioux Indian brave with a knife in his hand. She made the sign of the cross, knowing full well that this would be her doom. She stood frozen in place. The Indian motioned toward the bread. Mrs. Vanek stepped aside. The Brave made his way over to the fragrant loaf. He sliced it in half. He handed her one half and made his way off with the other half.

Grandma Vanek lifted her forefinger to her forehead, then her breast and from one shoulder to the other as she looked up at the sky saying, "*Jezis, děkuji.*"

Twenty Four

The successive years moved along uneventfully for Frank and his surrogate Bohemian family. Since his arrival, Anton and Sylvia added to their livestock with the introduction of pigs. With the addition of a chicken coop for the hens and frying chickens, Frank had another job of cleaning out the coop and adding straw to the nests. Having added ducks and geese, now there would be roast goose on the platter at Thanksgiving. This was a new holiday for Frank as the Europeans had not observed this day. He rather liked the thought of thankfulness for the year's harvest. He heard that other neighbors had relatives over to feast together, but, even though the neighbors were friendly with the Houbovys, people didn't usually come by to visit like he would have enjoyed. This made him lonely for his family back in the old country. He wondered why no one ever came to call socially. Anton and Sylvia were friendly and nice enough.

There wasn't anyone he could ask without feeling he would be betraying his kind employers if word got around that he was curious. It might have something to do with their son being missing. This mystery nagged at him. Perhaps, there were some things one should never know.

Only in idle times did he miss his parents and family. Only in idle times did he fret about not knowing where Anton and Sylvia's son was. Did he go off the deep end and did they have to send him to a hospital in Lincoln to get well? Did he kill someone and get sent to prison in Lincoln? Funny how no one ever talked about it.

He had his own worries, though, always concerned that the authorities would discover that he snuck on board the ship to America without going through the proper process. He thought about how lucky he was when his Aunt Josepha tucked her little one under her billowy skirt so that he could count as a family member. He worried whenever he heard a stranger was in town and could that stranger be looking for him, ready to send him back? He had been here now for one half of the year of 1885, all of 1886 and now 1887 was about to come to an end as well. Surely, if they were looking for him they would have found him by now.

As thoughts came and went through his mind, Frank also began to think about one day finding a woman who would be his wife and give him children. They would need children, a lot of children, to help on the farm he planned to own. Where would he find her? Would she be as beautiful as his mother? Would she be kind and gentle, yet strong enough to help with the farm work? Where would he find a lady that could cook as well as his own mother? Frank wasn't a religious young man – one that would resort to praying for such a person to come into his life. But then, what could it hurt? He didn't even know how to pray that well except for the memorized words his mother taught him at bedtime when he was little. As she sat in her rocking chair, he would kneel in front of her and recite Otcenas before going to bed.

With the thoughts drifting in and out of his consciousness, he drifted off and let go of his worries, not thinking so fervently for a long time after.

Twenty Five

The day began as any ordinary day for the young apprentice farmer. Christmas and New Year's had passed with only a modicum of fanfare on the eastern plains of Butler County, Nebraska. The weather was unusually balmy for Thursday, the twelfth of January in 1888. A soft fluffy snow covered the ground, but not enough to hamper taking the cows down to the river bank to graze on the grasses that hadn't yet perished under the cloak of winter. The young immigrant from Bohemia was making his way as a hired hand and cow herder.

Farmers along the way were out in the fields in shirt sleeves. Others had their cattle out in the fields. He passed by the one room school house on the way noticing the children frolicking outside at recess not wearing any coats. He had only worn a lightweight jacket himself. Situating his herd about a quarter mile from the farmstead, Frank pulled the harmonica out of his pocket. By now, his Holsteins had become accustomed to hearing his lively tavern tunes as they noshed and chewed their cuds along the bank. Even the water of Oak Creek was still running unfettered under only a sliver of ice.

Frank noticed that the herd was particularly antsy that morning. They walked reluctantly on the path they had taken many times before and his lead cow, Bossy, was especially nervous. Frank wasn't sure what to make of this. He had seen them act strangely in the summer time before a thunderstorm, but never like this.

As his tunes drifted through the air, at one point, Bossy actually turned her head around and looked back at the herder as if to say, "Why aren't you paying any attention to me?" His stock didn't seem to be the least interested in eating. Generally, it took extra effort to keep them out of the creek grasses. Today was different. Then as though Bossy had given a command to her underlings, down they went.

"What's going on with you guys?" Frank yelled at them. "Get up, get up. This isn't the time to be lazy," he commanded them.

How could he have been so forgetful by leaving his shepherd's crook behind? He foraged around looking for something else to prod Bossy to get up, so the rest would follow her lead.

As Frank foraged to find a stick, he looked to the northwest. Looming before him was a vast, ominous-looking cloud that seemed to have appeared out of nowhere.

"Come on Bossy, get up. Get up. We have to get home."

Frantically, he decided he would go right up to her and blow his harmonica right into her ear. It worked. With her front legs kneeling under her, she raised up her hind legs and turned toward home. Simultaneously the rest of the brood followed her lead and got to their feet.

"Good girl, Bossy, good girl," Frank praised.

As with fierce vengeance, the wind suddenly turned to the north and began whipping the snow from the ground into his face. The gusts were so strong it blinded his eyes making it seem as though his eyelids were glued shut. Balmy temperatures gave way to a ferocious drop in temperature.

I didn't come all the way over the ocean to have a snow storm do me in, he thought. "Come Bossy, help us get home."

Frank latched on to Bossy's tail. He hung on with all his might, despite the vicious and bitterly cold wind and snow. She began to walk faster and faster, almost in a run. Frank stumbled on a rock falling to the ground, yet managing to hang on to the mangy part of her bony tail. Bossy was bound for the barn with her convoy trotting behind. Together they struggled the distance that seemed unendingly piercing through the rapid, raging wind and snow.

Bossy and the herd streamed through the wide door of the barn, with Frank still clutching her tail. His mind was numb due to the severe cold. Once inside, his eyes peered out the door to see the house. There was one solid sheet of white, swirling snow. There was no way he could make it into the warmth of the fire Sylvia had burning in the kitchen stove. He would have to stay inside of the barn until the storm let up.

When his stiff, cold fingers began to feel circulation, Frank found the pitch fork and made a nest of straw where he'd try to keep warm for the duration. The wind continued to howl. He thought about how Anton and Sylvia would worry about him and the herd. He hoped that they had the good sense not to go out looking for them. As he looked at his pocket watch the hands showed 6:00 p.m. His stomach was growling and he began to get thirsty. The cows began to beller.

There were no buckets in the barn, yet the cows needed relief from their heavy utters. He began with Bossy, milking her by squirting the milk into his own mouth. It was warm and foamy. He needed to milk quickly so she wouldn't lose her milk. As quickly as he milked, he swallowed. This would need to be his nourishment until the storm let up. One by one, he milked the cows, letting the milk fall into the straw. It was a shame to waste it, but it couldn't be helped. Listening to unrelenting howling winds, Frank waited for the cows to lie down to sleep before he bedded down next to Bossy. Her energy kept him warm even though he only wore a light jacket.

Morning dawned but the storm raged on. He didn't know what to make of it. The previous winters hadn't been like this. As the cows began to moo, Frank began the same process he had before by first feeding himself and then milking the herd to relieve their pain. He hoped that Anton and Sylvia could hear the cows mooing from the barn, but with the never ending wind and the bitter cold, he figured they were trying to stay warm like everyone else. It had already been 12 hours since the storm set in. It couldn't go on forever.

Frank slid the barn door open only a crack to look out. All was still white with no sign of the house. He could smell the smoke from their chimney, so that was comforting knowing they were burning coal and staying warm.

He was on his third round of milking which kept him from too much discomfort. He looked at his watch once more. He might as well play a tune for the ladies for providing him with his supper. He bedded down once more with Bossy and hoped that morning would bring an end to the raging blizzard.

"Oh, thank God, you made it back," Sylvia shrieked at the door when she saw Frank stumble in. "And you managed to get the herd back. You could have frozen out there, you know." she said as she threw a warm blanket around him.

Frank was destined to live – he and his herd of milk cows. Many others weren't that fortunate. The blizzard that ravaged the Nebraska plains on January 12, 1888 took an estimated 230 people according to the Butler County Banner that came out the following week. Sadly, the majority of the deaths were that of children trapped in the schools, unprepared. With not enough fuel to stay warm, many froze to death. With temperatures that hit 30 and 40 degrees below zero, few could have predicted such a horrible disaster.

Upon reading the reports, ugly stories emerged how people's eyelids tore as they froze shut. People collapsed a short distance from their doorsteps due to the hurricane force winds that whipped new and existing snow.

What was unbelievable was that it could have been 30 to 40 degrees above zero in the morning and plummeted to 30 to 40 degrees below zero by

2:00 p.m. It didn't just blow through, it raged for 18 hours.

Anton and Sylvia praised the young cow herder they had taken under their wing, "You had the good sense, young man, to know what it took to survive, and you managed to save our herd as well."

"No, Anton, Bossy was the one who saved the herd and me."

The following pay day, Frank learned his wage was increased to $1.00 per day.

Twenty Six

It took some time for everyone to recover from the devastation of the blizzard. Folks mourned the losses of loved ones as well as those who lost livestock. Anton and Sylvia were grateful beyond measure that their herd was safe, but more importantly, they were thankful that Frank made it back safely. He had become like a second son to them and they could not have coped with losing another one.

From that time on, the farmers watched the skies more closely. The post office saw a rise in deliveries of the Farmer's Almanac. The word got around that the Almanac would foretell weather patterns, helping the farmers plan. Anton and Sylvia eagerly awaited their issues of the Farmer's Almanac to such a degree they used it as a guide for planting as well.

Frank did not have long to wait to own his own property. This would mean he would need the necessities: a horse with harness and a plow. Anton told him he could continue to stay there and still work for them even after he got his first parcel. Frank had his eye on land that lay near where Oak Creek and Skull Creek forked. Skull Creek was so named because of the Pawnee Tribe skulls left along its banks when the settlers first saw the area. Frank had his eyes on an artesian well on the property which would be valuable for watering his own herd one day and digging a well would be easier if the water table was high.

Frank often counted the money he'd saved in an old brown envelope that the Farmer's Almanac came in, one that Sylvia was going to throw away. He counted the one dollar bills he had earned since he started. He had managed to save almost every bit of the $750.00. It was the most money he had ever had in his young life. Frank kept the money under the straw mattress. The Farmers' Bank had not opened yet. He thought about where the safest place was to keep it. *If anything happened to this money I'd have to start all over again.*

"There's a farm sale next week. You can take time to come along if you want to," Anton said to Frank.

"I've been thinking that I need to buy a horse and if they have a plow, I can get that too, if it goes cheap enough for me," Frank replied.

"They usually get $25.00 for a good horse," Anton said. "A plow will probably run about $10.00.

Frank figured he would take about $50.00 out of his savings for the sale. He was getting excited thinking about being able to get a horse. He'd be able to ride it as well. Frank had been wanting to check out more of the surrounding countryside and after the evenings got long, he would have time to do that. He remembered that he would also need a bridle and harness as well. He'd better take out $100.00.

The day of the farm sale came and the three of them hitched up the wagon and headed out. It was a warm day for the middle of May. Every so often they heard the trill of a meadow lark. As they drove the wagon along the Creekside, mourning doves sang their mournful song.

"Will you help me figure out if the horse is healthy or not before I bid on it?" Frank asked Anton.

"I'll show you what I know about the age of a horse by looking at its teeth," Anton said.

It was around 10:00 a.m. when they got to the farm sale. Yet another family was giving up on prairie life. They had lost children in the blizzard and needed to find a different life in order to cope with their losses. They would be eager to sell, yet people from all around didn't want to take advantage of them either. So they offered reasonable prices for their items.

Sylvia went over to look at the household goods while the menfolk went directly over to the four horses corralled near the barn.

"Come over here, Frank," Anton said as he lifted the first horse's upper lip. We can tell a lot by the angle of the teeth as to how old this guy is." Then he lifted the lower lip and said, "He has teeth that line up, so that's good. If the teeth are milky white you know he is five years old or under. When their teeth get yellowish, they are between five and twenty." He lifted the upper lip again, even though the horse didn't like it that much. "Easy boy, let's look for the seven-year hook on the upper corner. That will indicate his age pretty close. You can generally tell by looking at the animal if it's healthy and also if the breath is not bad."

After everyone had a chance to examine the livestock, the auctioneer began his program. "You'll have to help me with the bidding," Frank told Anton.

"Who'll give me $15.00?" the auctioneer went on with his fast talk.

Frank shot his hand in the air. That would be a steal, he thought.

"I've got $15.00, who'll give me $20.00?" the man shouted.

"Twenty here," a man called out.

"Who'll give me $25.00?"

Frank raised his hand again, yelling out $25.00.

The other bidder did not raise him as he heard the Auctioneer say, "Sold to the young man for $25.00."

Frank was excited. He now owned his very own draft plow horse who was black in color with white socks, mane and tail with a white facial blaze. *I think I'll rename him Noc, meaning night.*

When the bidding was over for the livestock, they started in on the tack for the horses. Frank had scouted out the harness that the farmer had used on Noc. It was just a matter of bidding on it. He was able to get the harness with detachable bridle for $5.00. Later, he bid on the plow at $10.00 and got it. Anton taught him well about going prices.

It had been a successful day for Frank. It was daunting to realize he now had another mouth to feed beside himself. He liked that he would be able to use the bridle separately for his rides exploring the countryside.

They loaded the wagon with the plow, harness and items that Anton and Sylvia bought. Frank had never bridled a horse before. The farmer came over and showed him how. He hoped Noc would like him. "I'll have to start talking to you so we become friends," he said to his new ride.

Twenty Seven

Noc fit right in with Anton's draft horses. Frank quickly learned how to bridle him and even though he had no saddle, he would ride him bareback as he had seen others do.

Sylvia, like all the others in the area, baked a lot of bread. They got the flour from the grocery store that in turn got the flour from the largest mill in the country at the time in Minnesota. They were fortunate to have it brought in by rail. There was talk among neighbors that Brainard would be getting a flour mill of their own soon. Sylvia was pleased to hear that.

Frank was eager to ride into town on a slow day when the cattle were in the corral and not in need of herding. "If you'll give me a pillow case to carry the things in, I'll ride to the store and get your flour. I'll take Noc. They have hitching posts in front, so it should work out just fine for me. I'll let

Kamos tag along too. We'll make a time of it," Frank said to Sylvia.

"See if we have any mail while you're there," she replied.

Sylvia had given him money for the supplies and a few other things she needed. When he finished up at the store, he asked to leave his purchases at the end of the corner while he went to the post office.

Reaching into their mail box with his big hands, he was delighted to see they had mail. Upon further examination, his hands trembled as he recognized a small, wrapped package in brown paper with his name on it. At last! It was the reply to his letter he had long awaited. He didn't want to open it right there. He tucked it under his arm as he hurried back to the grocery store. *What could they have they sent? It felt like something in it was hard.*

Frank reached the store where Noc and Kamos patiently waited. Frank had used the same methods of training a dog as they did in Bohemia where the animal always knew that his master was truly the master. Whoever trained Noc used the same technique.

Tucking the mail along with his package into the pillowcase, along with the sack of flour, he carefully slung it over the horse's neck as he mounted, took hold of the reins, and with a double click of his tongue, they were heading home. All along their steady stride home, Frank mused as to what could be in his package from home.

The short ride took forever it seemed, but at last they arrived. Frank dismounted, as Kamos ran over to his water bowl. He took the pillowcase off of Noc's neck and led him to the corral for water as well.

"That didn't take you long," Sylvia said. "I thought you'd poke around longer."

"Look at what came in the mail," Frank said showing her his package.

They both went inside where he proceeded to the kitchen table immediately. He reached into his pocket for his trusted knife and cut the cord that held the package together. As he carefully unwrapped his treasure, a letter fell onto the table along with an envelope and something wrapped again very carefully. As he took off the inner wrapping, he discovered the ceramic pipe. It was the one his father always smoked at the pool hall on Sundays when they drank beer, laughed, and listened to music.

"Why would they be sending me this?" he said to Sylvia.

"Read the letter and find out."

Frank began to read.

Dear Franta,

It was thoughtful of you to leave a note on your pillow so we would know where you went. Your father missed you terribly. I have missed you too, yet I can understand why you needed to go to America. You had to follow your dream. That is where the money is to be made and you don't have to go into the draft like here.

I am sending you your father's ceramic pipe. He would have wanted you to have it. A few months after you left, your father began coughing terribly. It got worse and worse and he didn't want me to call in a doctor. Finally I did, but it was too late to help him. He passed on in the morning of March 16. He always wanted to stay here because of his Maminka, and here he passed on before she did. I asked her to move in with me so it isn't so lonely.

I hope you are doing well over there. Write often. Maybe you can come back and visit yet while I am still alive.

Milovat,
Maminka

Sylvia knew from the sad face that Frank had that he had received bad news. "Is there anything you'd like to say?" she asked him.

"I can't believe it. I expected him to live forever." With those words he gathered up the pipe and letter and walked upstairs to be alone.

Twenty Eight

Frank awakened the next morning still clutching the letter from his mother. He hadn't remembered crying since he was a small child when he skinned his knees after falling down. Last night he let the tears flow. He mourned the loss of his father, but in addition his burst of grief was a compilation of leaving his parents and his homeland, the stress associated with sneaking on board ship, then wondering what would come next and how he would make it. He managed to keep a stiff upper lip all this time, but the news of his father's passing was more than his mind could endure. He wished he was near his mother where she could comfort him and he, in turn, could comfort her. He could not let this keep him down. Anton and Sylvia were expecting him to continue on with his work. With that thought in mind, he rose to go downstairs. He couldn't look back. He had to be grateful for what he had going for him and push onward.

"Good morning, Frank," Sylvia said as he moved to take his place at their breakfast table. "We are so very sorry you lost your father," they said almost simultaneously.

"It hit me hard, but I'll be alright. You have work for me to do. I am more determined than ever to do well so wherever *Táta* is, he'll be proud of me," Frank replied.

They ate their oatmeal in silence that morning after that brief conversation. Frank went out to milk the cows and on to do his routine chores. Nothing more about his father's death was mentioned again.

That evening Frank brought his mother's package downstairs in order to read by the kerosene lamp. He opened the sealed envelope she had enclosed. In the front was written "tobacco seeds". Frank remembered watching his father plant tobacco. It looked fairly easy at the time, but this was different.

"Sylvia, do you have use for that little box over there?"

"No, I was going to burn it in the stove. Would you like to have it?"

"*Maminka* sent me some of *Táta's* tobacco seeds. I wondered if I could start them in the house and later put them in a shady spot behind the barn."

"It will be fun if they start. The seeds are so tiny, I can hardly see them," Sylvia said.

"I know. I'll have to be very careful not to lose any since I don't know where I'd find any other. Besides, I want to make my father's tobacco grow now that I have his pipe."

The next day, Frank filled the box with loose soil and sprinkled some water on it to moisten the dirt. He was remembering how his father did it. He took some of the teeny, tiny seeds and laid them on top of the soil. "Care if I put it on the window sill?" he asked her.

"That will be fine. Do you want to use this little sprinkler I use in the kitchen to water them each day, so the seeds don't wash away to the edge?" Sylvia added.

The warmth of the sun shining into the kitchen window worked well to germinate the seeds. Each day they all checked to see if they could see anything green. On the seventh day, it happened. A little green leaf was peeking through the dirt. Each day, another would pop up. Frank was happy. Now, all he had to do was to let them grow some more and put them into something bigger before he was ready to put the seedlings into the ground in the chosen spot.

"My father used to put something on top of the plants to help them grow, but I don't know what that was," Frank said to Anton.

"I'll ask around and see if I can find out. Old Man Tuba knows a lot about things, maybe he'll know," Anton said.

Frank came in from the evening milking one day as Anton greeted him with a sack with something in it. "Go ahead, look inside," Anton said.

Frank opened the sack and looked in. "Whew, smells awful!" he said.

"Old Tuba said he makes it up from ground alfalfa that has fermented. Tobacco likes nitrogen and that's what he uses to grow his." Anton said.

"Well, if it works for him, I'll give it a try," Frank said closing the sack and storing it on the back porch. "Now, don't you dig in this, Kamos," he cautioned his dog. "Everything I have to grow this tobacco is scarce. I can't make any mistakes."

After supper was over, Frank worked up the soil so his plants would be ready. He waited until all danger of frost was over and then planted the seedlings. "I'm not a religious man, but this time I might think of saying a prayer to *Jezis, Maria.*"

Twenty Nine

"I see some fine green leaves up in your tobacco patch, Frank."

Sylvia was right. His crop was peeking out of the ground. He was thrilled. "Now, if I can just keep the rabbits from eating it," he said to her.

It took some care for the tender plants to reach some height. In a few weeks it seemed they would make it. His next worry was that they didn't get a hail storm.

That afternoon when Frank rode Noc into town to see if they had mail, he noticed a stranger across the street from the Post Office. Fear gripped him as he turned the horse around and rode back home. The mail run could wait until tomorrow. He wasn't going to risk being asked any questions. He wondered if this fear would ever leave. He hated always looking over his shoulder, even in this little village. *I've come too far to get sent back now.*

The next day he tried again to get the mail. While at the post office he asked the Postmaster if he had seen the stranger and did he know what he wanted.

The post master told him he was a surveyor plotting some land for the railroad. Frank relaxed.

"There's sure a lot of talk about the election coming up in November. Everything is going along just fine, so I see no sense in changing presidents," the postmaster said.

"I don't know much about either Cleveland or Harrison," Frank replied. "I guess I should pay better attention. So long as we stay out of war, that's all I care about."

Frank mounted Noc, who he'd become as attached to about as much as Kamos. He mounted his ride and rode back to the farmstead with the supplies Sylvia had asked him to buy.

He hadn't heard from his mother again after she wrote about his father's death. He worried about her being alone with his grandmother. He couldn't allow his thoughts to linger even though the grief of losing his father followed him everywhere – herding the cows, milking the cows, riding into town – a constant companion, especially it was there when he laid his head down to sleep. He wondered if this heaviness would ever leave him.

That night upon retiring to his little attic room, Frank removed his mother's letter to reread it. As he lifted the mattress, just as he had done many times before, he spotted some paper tucked farther in underneath. He reached as far as his arm would allow and pulled out a brown envelope. Inside were papers with large, bold print. Frank's English wasn't proficient, yet he could make out most of it.

Wanted!
Laborers to Complete the Southern Pacific Railroad.
Good Wages, Room and Board
Age 18 to 30
Must be strong and of sound mind
Need to sign contract to work
until completion
Hop on the next train west
for the Adventure of a lifetime!

Frank could read enough of it to make out that this is probably where Anton's and Sylvia's son had gone. *But why would he go without saying a word? Was there more to the story then they told me? Why am I questioning the son's leaving when I did the same thing* myself? But, my case was different. I had to come across the ocean.

He held the paper in his hand, slapping it against the other hand as he thought about it. Should he take it downstairs and show it to Anton and Sylvia, or should he leave well enough alone? Frank decided to sleep on it and think it over more when he was out herding the cows. He wished he had Peter to talk this over with. If only he could find out where Peter was so he could at least write to him. Now, he had two things to think about.

Thirty

"You're awfully quiet, Frank," Sylvia said at breakfast.

"Can't help thinking about my mother and grandmother now that my father is gone."

"I see," she said as she busied herself at the stove and didn't press him any further.

Frank was eager to go out with his herd that day. He mounted Noc and called for Kamos to come along. He'd have time to turn over all the different possibilities in his mind. What would his mother tell him to do? She would say he should tell them about the paper he found. What would his father say he should do? He would tell him to leave it alone and let it play itself out. He wasn't any farther from a decision than when he started. Then he remembered the saying his father always used, "Why do things the easy way when the hard way will work?" His father used this adage as a joke when he saw someone doing a task without thinking.

Frank decided that he didn't want this weighing heavily on his mind, so that evening at supper, he would tell the couple what he found and let them figure out if that is where their son went. Even now, he felt a great burden lifted from his shoulders.

After doing his evening chores and washing up for supper, Frank went upstairs to get the paper he had found. He placed it into his overall pocket. He would wait until they were through with eating to show it to them.

Sylvia had made his favorite chicken dinner that night. She browned it in an iron skillet on the stove, seasoned it with caraway seed from her garden, and then put it into the oven to tenderize it. Frank's favorite piece was the breast. Anton liked the breast too, but Sylvia chose the drumsticks. She was a good cook, but then he remembered that all of the women in his family were good cooks. Each generation passed their skills on down to the next.

"That was my favorite meal, Sylvia," Frank said.

"She knows I like it too. There isn't anything she can't cook," Anton said as he leaned over to caress her shoulder.

"I have something to show the two of you," Frank said. "I found it when I was putting my letter away under the mattress. I don't know why I never saw it before, but anyway, I thought you should see it. It might give you some idea where you son is."

Sylvia reached for her glasses as Anton slid his chair over to read over her shoulder. They looked at each other and then they both gazed out the window as if in deep thought.

"There is an address at the bottom in smaller print. Do you think we should write to them, Anton?" Sylvia said.

"I guess it wouldn't hurt to write to at least find out if he is safe."

"Maybe, he will think we are meddling in his life. Remember, the scene we had with him the night before he left?" Sylvia said.

The next evening, when they were in the barn milking, Sylvia told the story of how Ivan came to them saying he didn't want to be a farmer the rest of his life. His father told him he was needed here and that in a few years he could go pursue his dream. They argued about it back and forth, and finally Ivan just threw his arms up and went to bed. The next day he wasn't here to help with the chores or herd the cattle. This was just a short time before you came to see if we needed a hired man. She told how Anton felt terrible that they had quarreled and wished that he could take it back and just give him his blessing and tell him to go, which he did anyway.

Frank listened intently and wondered how much he had hurt his own parents when he ran away as he did. At least he let them know where he was so they could get in touch with him. That was some consolation to his conscience.

They must have decided to wait and not check on him. Their instincts told them Ivan was safe and just too ashamed to get in touch with them. They would continue to pray for at least a letter from him.

The summer wore on hot and humid as usual. Some nights, Frank thought that sleeping in the attic room was unbearable. He made a plan that he would go to the next sale and see if he could find a cot he could sleep on outside on those stifling nights. The next time he went to get the mail, he would read the bulletin board of items people had for sale and see if he could find one.

The hot nights did one thing that was positive. They made the tobacco grow. Frank rode Noc over to Old Man Tuba's house to get information on how to harvest his crop and brought him back with him.

"Well, let me see what you have here son," the old man said to Frank. "Looks like a mighty fine crop for your first growing."

"It was most likely that alfalfa mixture you gave me that gave it a good start," Frank replied.

"It's ready for cutting. You got a hand scythe somewhere?" Tuba asked.

Frank went to the tool shed and fetched the scythe. Old Man Tuba showed him how to cut the stalks and lay them on the ground to be bundled with twine. "There are several ways of curing the 'baccy, but my way of doing it is air drying. You could fire cure it, but that takes a special barn. You could sun dry it, but the easiest for me is to air dry it."

They bundled about ten leaves together and tied them with twine. The crop produced about 20 bundles that they hung up from the rafters in the barn. They'd need to let them dry about six to eight weeks to cure. "That'll about be the end of September. When the time is up, come and get me again, and I show you how to ferment it. In the meantime, order yourself a tobacco grinder from Sears & Roebuck catalog."

"I didn't realize there was so much to growing your own tobacco," Frank said.

"It seems like a lot the first time you do it, but the 'baccy will last you quite a while and it will smoke sweeter than that you buy out of a can, and it's practically free, except for the time and effort.

"After this, you can show me how to make *pivo*," Frank laughed.

"I can do that. You're mighty young to be taking up vices like drinking beer, wouldn't you say?"

Frank eagerly waited for the end of September to roll around so he could get Mr. Tuba back to show him the rest of the tobacco process.

"I brought you some gunny sacks to put the tobacco leaves into. We need to ferment them to take the ammonia out of it. We're going to let the tobacco sweat by putting the bundles in the bags and letting them get to about 140 degrees. You'll need to turn them occasionally so the tar, ammonia and nicotine are released. You wouldn't want to smoke it without doing this. We're getting closer all the time. After it's done fermenting, I'll show you how to strip it. That's when you'll need the grinder."

"Thanks, Mr. Tuba. I never paid enough attention to how my father did it when I was back home. He always got together with my uncle and they grew and processed it together."

When the fermented leaves were ready, Mr. Tuba showed Frank how to strip the leaf from the stem. You had to be careful not to let it crumble.

By the time the leaves were fermented, the tobacco grinder came through the mail. Sylvia said, "It looks a lot like my coffee grinder."

Tuba and Frank worked together in the cool of the evening when his work was finished. They stripped each leaf carefully, putting them into a pan until they'd start grinding.

"You'll want to figure out the setting on the grinder to see how coarse or how fine you want it, but I'll show you how I like it," Tuba said.

When all was done, Frank brought out his father's ceramic pipe. Tuba showed him how to tamp it into the bowl. He also showed him how to strike a kitchen match by lifting his leg and dragging it over his rump down to his hip. Amazingly, Frank got it to light.

"Easy does it," Tuba said. "Don't want to go crazy on it right off." Frank took his first puff. It tasted sweet. It smelled sweet. It reminded him of his father. All of a sudden his lungs began to feel like they were burning. He began to sputter and cough. He coughed until he bent over. This wasn't as pleasant as he had imagined it.

"I told you to go easy. You're not used to it. Let me try a little and see if it's ready," Tuba said. He tamped some into his own pipe, lit the match and took a little puff. "Sweet, just like we like it. It'll just take some time for you to get used to it."

After Mr. Tuba left, Frank packed his tobacco away, took out what was in the bowl, and put his pipe away. Maybe another day.

Thirty One

The next farm sale Anton and Frank went to, Frank found a steel coiled cot with springs so he could throw a quilt over it and get some sleep on those hot, humid nights in the summertime. The farmer did have a mattress to fit it, but most likely it wasn't designed to have a mattress since the springs were tightly woven springs and served well for temporary bedding.

He loved laying out under the stars, looking at the Milky Way, the Big Dipper and at times, since they were north enough in the hemisphere, even the Northern Lights were visible. An occasional comet would streak through the sky. Lying there alone with the world around him with only the star-studded sky, he wondered what it will be like to share his space with a young lady. He never went anywhere socially so he'd have a chance to meet one. This was beginning to weigh heavily on his mind. Frank wasn't one to leave things to chance, so he lay there devising a plan as to how he could mingle with some people his own age. He often noticed loving glances Anton and Sylvia gave one another. Then when it rained, they often said they were tired and retired earlier than usual.

The rooster woke Frank at the break of dawn. He splashed cold water on his face, dressed for the day, and went to the barn for morning milking before he went in for breakfast.

As he approached the corral, he noticed something peculiar. Noc was rolling around on the ground and kicking at his stomach.

"Hurry, Anton, hurry. Something's wrong with Noc," he shouted.

Anton was half dressed as he pulled the straps of his overalls up over his shoulders.

"Did he get out on the alfalfa?" Anton asked.

"Not at all. He was noshing on some grass along the bank as I was herding. Do you suppose he got into some bad grass?"

"Run and get Old Man Tuba. He has remedies for everything," Anton said.

Mr. Tuba was just finishing his breakfast when Frank arrived breathlessly. Frank told him what was going on and without hesitation, the old man ran out to the barn returning carrying a liniment bottle, a beer bottle, and some other liquid.

"It's just as quick to hoof it rather than taking time to hitch up the wagon," he told Frank. They hurried over as Frank's heart raced wildly. *I hope he can help him. I don't know what I'd do if I lost him now that I've gotten to know Noc and we're so close.*

"Most likely he has colic or gas," Mr. Tuba told Frank. "You talk real calm to him in his face so he doesn't roll, and I'll stick this bottle in the side of his mouth and get this tonic down his throat. When it reaches his belly, you'll hear the biggest fart you've ever heard," Tuba said.

"I hope so. I don't want to lose you, old buddy, nor the money I paid for you," Frank said every so kindly as Tuba poured the medicine down him.

Noc lay there for a minute longer, then got up and walked around a bit.

"Walk him. That will help too," Tuba said as Anton and Sylvia stood by. Tuba was right. It wasn't long and you could hear Noc sputtering with each step he took. They walked and walked. "Don't let him eat for a while, but he can have water," Tuba said as Frank led him to the stock tank.

"What do I owe you?" Frank asked the self-proclaimed veterinarian.

"Not one darn thing, unless of course, you want to part with some of that there pipe 'baccy," he grinned.

"I'll go get you some," Frank said.

"I suppose he knows what made the horse sick?" Tuba said to Anton.

"We're not sure, but he thinks it was some grass while he was herding cows," Anton told him.

Frank came out with a container with his tobacco. "Here you go. I sure thank you."

"Think nothing of it. I just hope he stays well."

Thirty Two

After the scare of almost losing his horse, Frank realized, for the first time, how quickly life can change. He reflected on events. He had learned of his father's death only a short time earlier. Then, Noc took sick - feeling the possibility of losing him too. Up to now, he thought mainly about his own survival and forging ahead with his goals. Suddenly, he realized there were others to consider, and that he alone was not the center of the universe.

Old Man Tuba lived alone a few miles from Anton & Sylvia's farm. Frank thought he should exercise Noc on Sunday afternoon, so they took a ride out to Mr. Tuba's. As they rode up the lane, Noc began to balk with his ears back and not wanting to continue. Was he reminded of the time Tuba poured tonic down his throat?

"Easy Boy. That's okay. Tuba's a good guy. He made you well," Frank consoled him. With a slow gait, they approached. From out on the porch came strains of music.

"I know what you're anxious about. That's an accordion we're hearing," Frank told Noc. "Better get used to this, old boy."

There sat Old Man Tuba actually playing a tuba. On approach, Frank spotted the accordion man he had seen on board ship. He leaped from his horse and said, "Is that really you?" The trombone and trumpet players kept on going with the old man oom-pa-pa-ing right along.

Joe set his four-row button accordion on the porch rocker and came to Frank as he hitched Noc to a post.

"How did you end up here?" Frank asked the accordion man. "Last time I saw you was on board ship."

"Someone told me the railroad had work. I took a job with them out of Omaha and now I'm making a run that brings me through Brainard," the young man said. "What are you doing here?"

Frank replied, "I saw a paper advertising farm land, but I found out I can't buy any until I'm 18. I have to wait.

"I see. I'll be coming through here twice a month."

"How did you know where Old Man Tuba lives?" Frank asked.

"News travels fast through the music world. Do you know his name isn't really Tuba? Everyone just calls him that because he's so good at the tuba. What do you play?"

A little embarrassed, Frank said shyly, "Oh, I try a tune on the harmonica."

"Nothing wrong with that. By the way, I don't know if you remember, but my name is Joe. Funny how we were all crammed in together on that ship and yet we never learned each other's names. Guess we figured we'd never see each other again, but here we are."

"They called me Franta on the ship, but my American name is Frank. I hope I can hear you play polkas every time you're through here."

They walked on over to the porch and Joe picked up his accordion and joined in.

Frank said to the band, "You guys are good, but if I played, I could do even better," and they all laughed at his wry humor.

Old Man Tuba offered everyone some of his homemade beer. Frank turned it down. "I don't want to take any chances of drinking before I'm 21. I don't want them to have any reason to deport me."

"Why would they deport someone who is working and good for the country?" Joe said.

"Since I came without any papers or as they say 'undocumented,' I can't take any chances. I don't have long to wait until I'm 21. I'd rather be safe than sorry," he replied.

From the time Frank came to America, he worried about being "found out". His uncle had instilled this fear in him right from the start when he saw him on board ship. It wouldn't be long now since everyone tells him that after five years, or when he applies for naturalization, he will be safe from having to constantly look over his shoulder.

Listening to the music, Frank was reminded of the days he spent with his father in the tavern back in the old country. He was glad he came and would come again.

Thirty Three

Anton grew his herd of cows to twelve. Frank had three more to watch over, but now that he had Noc, it was easier. Kamos helped keep them in check and out of unwanted grass. Anton and Sylvia were talking about ordering some material to string barbed wire around the pasture.

"Do you think we can set the posts and string wire?" Anton asked Frank.

"You're the boss. If you tell me how to do it, I'm sure we can fence those ladies in," Frank said. "I'd be free to help you with other things around here."

"We need to dig another hole for the privy. This is always an unfavorable job, but it has to be done at some time soon," Anton said.

"I started shoveling coal when I was eleven, so I can shovel dirt too. How deep a hole do we need to make?"

"Standard is usually 8 feet deep. I'm going to need a posthole digger for the fence posts anyway, so when I get that, we can use the posthole digger to loosen up the ground. It usually rains pretty well in August, so I'm thinking we can wait until the ground is softer to start. We can use the dirt to cover up the old one. Then I need to figure out a way to move the outhouse from the old sight over the new hole."

Sylvia used to throw the stove ashes down the privy to keep the odor down. She put cabbage and other vegetable peelings down there to help it compost and keep the stench away. They talked about the day that farms would have indoor toilets like the city folks back East have. That was a ways off for farmers in Butler County, Nebraska.

Anton had already ordered the posts and wire for the fence when he talked to Frank about it. Frank was eager to do something different for a change even if it was digging a new backhouse hole.

The rains came just as Anton had predicted. The newly designated holiday called Labor Day was started in 1882, three years before Frank arrived. This was new to Frank, a day to honor the workers in the country. Brainard was starting to have little celebrations in town with a small parade and people getting together to eat. There was talk that one day it would grow into a special festival with bands.

A hint of autumn was in the air when Anton and Frank started on their digging project. Frank had never used a posthole digger before and found it to be a handy tool. This wasn't going to be an overnight job, so to speak. The cooler temperatures helped. Frank had folded up the metal cot he had been using to sleep on outside when it was hot upstairs in his room. His birthday had come and gone. He wondered if the years would always go this slowly. All the land he checked on through the Homestead Act had been claimed, so he would have to keep his eyes open for someone selling out or maybe the railroad would release some more of their land. He kept informed by watching the bulletin board at the post office and also at the railroad depot.

Some nights Frank lay awake thinking about all there was to do with being a farmer. In the old country, he and his father just went to work each day and did the same thing, then came home to rest, eat, sleep, and get ready for the next day. Here on the farm there was so much to think about and much planning to do what with the livestock to tend each day, day in and day out.

Someone always had to be here in the morning and at night to feed and milk. During the summer months, Sylvia milked the cows so the menfolk could work in the fields until dark. Planting corn took place in May. First they plowed the field and then they had to disk it to soften the dirt. Next came the harrowing to level the ground out and finally the planting. Anton got his seed corn by ordering it through a seed catalog. He also subscribed to the *Nebraska Farmer Newspaper*. Frank didn't know how to read English that well, but he did enjoy the illustrations. Just about anything the farmer needed could be ordered through mail order.

Anton had an established crop of alfalfa when Frank came to work for them. There was an early cutting and a later one. Alfalfa along with prairie hay was cut and then swept into rows to be stacked on a pile. Now that Anton had a barn, they would pitch it into the hay wrack and haul it to the barn where they heaved it with pitchforks into the hay loft. It then was released through special openings in the floor to drop down for feeding the cattle and horses. Newly mown hay had the most wonderful aroma. Anton cautioned Frank that they had to make sure the hay was good and dry before it was stored. Now and then they heard of a barn that burned down from spontaneous combustion caused by hay that was stored too wet.

The wheat and oat crops were sown year after year and were ready for harvesting usually in late June or early July. Frank remembered that the small farmers in Bohemia cut their grain with a hand sickle, but Anton had a mower now. He would go back over the cut grain and rake it into rows to be picked up by a binder that was put it into shocks. Anton, Sylvia and Frank, all three, would go out and bundle the wheat and oats and stack them into shocks to dry.

"This year when we come in from the fields, we'll have a shower to rinse the chaff off our bodies," Anton told Sylvia and Frank.

Anton took a tin drum he bought at a farm sale and filled it with water. He built a wrack to hold it into the air high enough for a grownup to stand under. He cut a hole in the barrel and put in a sprinkling can that could be opened with a petcock. The hot sun would heat the water enough so it wouldn't be too cold as it sprinkled down on them at the end of the day. Thankfully, the shocking didn't take but two or three days for the three of them to do. Sylvia's chickens enjoyed a shock of oats which she threw into the chicken pen for them to peck on. *Will I ever remember this all when I have my own place?*

The farmers in the area all helped each other out with the threshing. After the shocks were dry, the threshing crew came through the area and within a day the grain was gleaned and only straw was left. The straw came out of the threshing machine into a stack. Precious straw was used for various functions such as hens' nests in the chicken house. Sylvia also used straw to shield her strawberry bed from the hot sun and to keep the berries moist after she carried water on them.

They had scarcely finished with harvest when the second cutting of hay was upon them. There was little time to rest. Once again, they ate supper by lamplight. Frank could understand why Anton and Sylvia needed a hired hand. There was still no word from their son and Frank did not want to pry if they had tried to contact him.

Exhausted from working in the fields, Frank lay awake thinking about his mother. He formulated the words in his head of a letter he would write to her soon.

"There's a good farm sale I heard about," Anton said at supper one night. "Let's go see what is there we can't live without." When Saturday came, they hitched the team to the wagon and set off.

The farmer was selling out and moving on to work in the city. Frank's only purchase was a steel strong box. Now that he was accumulating earnings, he thought he should protect the money in case of fire. One just never knew what could happen. There was talk that Farmers Bank would soon open in Brainard, but until then, he needed to protect his earnings.

Anton bid on and bought a butchering trough. The hog was ready most any time. All they needed to wait for was cold weather. By November, it should be freezing enough that they can hang it up to cure. That would be another learning adventure for Frank.

Thirty Four

The day was crisp and cold, just the kind of day they needed for butchering a hog. It was mid-November so the bulk of the work would be finished by the Thanksgiving holiday. Not that the family ever had friends or relatives in, but for their own celebration, they wanted to have the mess over with. The weather had to be cold so the meat wouldn't spoil during the curing process.

Anton asked two of their closest neighbors – the ones he exchanged help with at times like when they put up the barn. He, in return, would help them butcher. The hog weighed about 300 pounds. They penned him separately and corn fed him the last few weeks. With four men, they should be able to string him up on the a-frame.

Frank had never watched or been part of this kind of a process. They had a huge pot in the yard where they piled wood around to heat the water for scalding the hog. Anton asked the neighbor to bring his 22 gage rifle. He was noted as an expert marksman and would shoot the hog between the eyes. Its throat was cut and one of the men held a large bowl under to catch the blood to be used for blood sausage. Then a horse pulled a slide that the hog was hoisted onto and taken over to the heated water pot. The water was dumped into the trough Anton bought at the farm sale. They all used sharpened knives to scrape the hide leaving the skin smooth. A metal gambrel meat hook was inserted into the hind legs so the hog could be hoisted by pulleys onto the a-frame. The scraping process took some time and even Sylvia came out to help with that.

"If you're at all squeamish, you won't want to watch as the hog's head is removed. It will be set aside to be used later," Anton told Frank.

"I may just as well face it right now so I know what to do when I have my own place, Frank said.

The process continued as Frank watched one of the neighbors, who was an expert butcher, cut the underbelly to remove the organs. The hog was rinsed as they splashed clean water on it. Then they let it cool.

Sylvia had prepared lunch for the men, but Frank had little appetite. He needed time to process what all had taken place. He wondered when the time came, if he would remember how to do this.

"You'll get to come and help when we butcher our hog," a neighbor said.

"That's what I need in order to get used to how this is done," Frank said.

"There's a lot more work yet in cutting up the hog and processing the lard," Anton said.

"Until you watch this, one doesn't really appreciate how that pork roast made it to the table," Frank replied.

Lots of people used to say, "Everything was used except the squeal." Frank believed it when he helped hold the intestines as Sylvia and Anton cleaned them by pouring a special salt-water brine through them over and over and inside out until they were clean. They would use these for jitrnice, the special bohemian sausage.

Frank wondered if it would taste as good as what his mother used to fry up for breakfast.

"We use the hog head, heart, kidneys, spleen and lungs. In addition I use raw liver, white bread, 6 cloves of garlic, salt, pepper, allspice, ginger, and marjoram. We grind the meat after it's been cooked and the fat trimmed away. I guess on the spices and taste until I get it just the way we like it. Then we stuff the casings, tie the ends with white string, and boil in the hot broth for about five minutes. We watch them carefully so the casing won't burst. Then we carefully remove each one from the broth and place in one inch of cool water," Sylvia told Frank.

"When I was a kid, I never paid much attention to how things were made. If I want to eat these after I'm married, I better pay close attention," Frank said.

"Married? That's the first time I've heard you say that. Is there someone we don't know about when you go off riding on Sunday afternoons?" Sylvia teased.

"No, not yet. I haven't had a chance to get to know any girls around here. As the town grows, I'm sure someone will come along," Frank said.

When the sausage making was done, they cut up the fat into cubes. Sylvia placed them in a black iron pan into the oven to cook. When the cracklings floated on top of the lard, she removed the pan and poured the lard into a bucket. She would save this in a crock to be used for many months in frying food. Anton cut the meat into squares that she roasted in the oven. When it was browned and tender, she put it into a large crock, then poured lard over it where it kept well into the spring. All she did was take a fork and dig out a few pieces, heat them up and the meat was ready for dinner.

Some people pickled pig's feet, but Sylvia never did. There wasn't much waste and what there was they buried out away from the house in a pit covered with dirt. As soon as they were finished, it was on to the next neighbor to help with the butchering there.

Thirty Five

Four weeks had passed since Anton salted down the slabs of ham in a crock so they could cure. A fire pit was built. Prior to the cold weather setting in, a 20 to 25 foot long, 2 foot deep trench was dug and covered with metal. Aluminum or galvanized metal could not be used because it would contaminate the smoke and the meat. The trench led from the fire pit to a 55 gallon drum. It was also built upslope to provide the proper draft. The drum barrel held rods that were placed inside to hold the slabs of cured pork. Dry wood and cobs at the bottom of the fire pit along with slightly green hickory, ash or oak was used to create smoke. Continuous smoke was necessary, thus the fire needed to be tended constantly. This process took two to three days of continuous smoking.

When Anton brought the first test slices for Sylvia and Frank to sample, their mouths salivated at the delicious taste. When the hams were finished, they wrapped them in butcher's paper and stored them in the cellar.

Hog butchering was not an easy or quick process, but the effort was worth it as the meat it provided served them throughout the year. The menfolk handled the bulk of the hog butchering, and Sylvia took care of dressing out a chicken or an occasional duck or goose. Along with the fresh vegetables from the garden and baked goods from the kitchen, the family ate well.

"There are few idle moments on the farm," Frank said to Sylvia. "It's not like when I went to work in the coal mine, then checked out and went home. Yet, I'm glad I came. I like this kind of life, even though I miss *Maminka*. I will write her about butchering a hog. She'll never believe it."

The cornfield was dry and ready for husking corn. They took a wagon with an extended bang board on the one side and the team of horses walked along slowly as all three of them pulled the ears of corn off the stalk and slung them into the wagon. They each had a corn pick on their thumb in order to cut the ear from the stalk. That bang board helped so they didn't overthrow the ears. Anton ordered some wire mesh that housed the corn since they didn't yet have a wooden corn crib. They shoveled the corn into the round crib, and then covered it with a canvas tarpaulin to keep it dry.

Frank thought about how there always was something different and new going on. Life never got dull on the farm. When the crops were in, their time and attention was turned to mending fences, repairing machinery, and tending the livestock.

As Frank climbed up the stairs for bed, he carried his strong box with him. Anton usually gave him a ten dollar bill and four singles for his week's pay. " Since crops are good and prices are up, I'm giving you a raise to $2.00 a day."

Frank shook Anton's hand until it nearly dropped off.

As Frank laid out his money on the bed, sorting it all out, he had close to $3700.00. *If they ever got the Farmers Bank built, I'd put this money in there,* he thought. Frank decided he would stow the strong box with cash in the cellar just in case the house burned or it got blown down by a tornado. There was no lock on the cellar door, but then, Anton and Sylvia never locked the house either. It was a toss-up.

Frank rode into town to get some things for Sylvia next day, and while he was at the grocery store, he would get some writing paper and envelopes. He needed to write to his mother again. He also decided to try to get in touch with Peter.

Even though he didn't have his address, they probably had a post office box in Brush Creek where they settled in Saline County. It would be worth a try, and if he didn't hear back, nothing was lost but a two cent postage stamp.

Frank walked into the grocery store and noticed two men dressed in suits and ties. It was too late to walk out unnoticed since Nellie called out to say hello. *I hope she doesn't try to make too much conversation,* he thought. The men made their purchase and walked out as Frank's heart beat fast.

"Federal Agents checking on land deals," Nellie said to Frank.

"Nice day, you having?" Frank said, quickly changing the subject.

He picked up the things on Sylvia's list. He wondered why she needed a can of lye and some borax. Stowing them in his bag, he then went over to the showcase to buy the stationery and envelopes.

"*Ja* need paper. Write *Maminka* in old country." Frank told her.

"That's nice of you to write to her. She'll be so pleased," Nellie said.

When Frank walked out the door, Nellie said to herself, *he's going to make a good husband one day.* Frank didn't seem the least bit interested in her. Perhaps, it was because she was not Bohemian. They seemed to marry their own nationality.

Frank checked to see if they had any mail, and all that was there was the Nebraska Farm Journal. He was recognizing a few more English words and enjoying the pictures. He mounted Noc and turned toward home.

"This may not be any of my business, Sylvia, but I'm wondering what you're needing lye and Borax for." he asked.

Our soap supply is getting low and when I get the chance, I'm going to make soap. "Didn't your mother make her own soap?"

"I think she did, but I never paid any attention to how she did it."

"I use my enameled pot and mix about four pounds of melted lard and two quarts of cold water together. Then I add one can of lye. I mix two tablespoons of Borax in a pint of water and add to the lye, water and lard mixture. Then I pour it into another enameled container and when it gets set, I cut it into bars."

After supper, Frank sat down with his new stationery and a pencil to write to his mother. So much had taken place since he wrote to her last. He harvested Táta's beautiful tobacco plants that grew from the seeds she sent him. He told how he tried it and coughed, so he'd wait until another time to try again. Perhaps he should not have taken such a deep drag on it, but only puffed. He told her about the accordion man and how they met up once again. He wrote, too, about how he gets nervous every time he sees strangers nosing around town. Then he told her about how they butchered the hog and made sausage. He knew she would be interested in how they harvested the corn crop. He asked his mother if she ever heard from Uncle Thomas's family and if so, to send their address to him. He wrote three pages. Any mother would have been delighted to get this letter. Folding the paper, he slipped it into the envelope and put six stamps on the envelope. This should take care of the ship's fees too, he hoped.

The next day, Frank rode into town with Kamos trotting behind. He took the letter over to the postal clerk and asked, "Do you think this will get there?"

"Looks like plenty of postage. It takes about three weeks, though."

This time there were no strangers lurking around to set his heart racing. He returned home.

Thirty Six

Winter came and went. It was time for spring planting again. It always pleased Frank to hear the Meadow Lark's trill on the prairie. Fencing in the pasture helped ease the monotonous task of herding the cows. Anton was teaching Frank most everything he needed to know when he would buy a place of his own. The May corn planting was over and all they needed now was to hope and pray heavy rains didn't wash it out.

Anton and Frank had scarcely come in from cultivating one afternoon when they noticed an ominously dark cloud over the western horizon.

"Hurry, let's get the livestock under cover. It looks like we're in for a good one," Anton shouted. They scurried around to get everything under wraps. Sylvia ran into the house to open all the windows so as to equalize the pressure if a tornado came through. The air was very still and the sky looked black and dark green. The animals were all fidgeting, so it seemed they sensed something. As soon as they secured everything, they climbed down the steps into the cellar. Anton kept an axe in the cave in case they were buried should the house fall on top of them. Sylvia kept fresh water in the cellar all summer. One could not be too well prepared. They had heard of several farmers who were saved when all their buildings were destroyed. No matter how well prepared they were, their hearts beat faster, especially at the thought of losing the livestock, their house and chickens. Sylvia made the sign of the cross and quietly said some Hail Mary's. Anton hung on to the rope that held the cover to the cave to peek out at what was going on. The wind was ferocious.

"Help me hang on to this," Anton shouted at Frank. "I can barely hold on to it." They waited out the storm as it whirled and howled above them.

This was Frank's first experience with a tornado even though he had heard many stories told about them. He heard that some storms could last up to an hour, but most generally, blew on by in about ten minutes. Anton could tell by the pressure on his hands holding the rope when it began to let up. As he cautiously opened the cellar door to look around, he saw that the house was still standing. The outer buildings were okay as well. Just then it came. Large stones falling from the sky. He quickly closed the lid again as they listened to when the hail would let up. It came in waves, it seemed: first with a vengeance, then a let up, and again with force. Finally, it let up enough for Anton to lift the cover. As he looked out over the yard, the ground looked as if it had snowed. He dropped the cover and sat on the top step and began to cry.

"What's wrong, Anton, what has happened?" Sylvia pleaded with him.

"Our corn is ruined! All that work and the expense of the seed," he said sobbing like a child.

Frank didn't know what to do or exactly what to say. Finally, he climbed up to him and said, "Don't worry, we'll get it planted again. I'll help pay for the seed corn."

Anton was taken back by Frank's generosity. "You can't spend the money you're saving for land," Anton said.

"You can repay me when the crop comes in," Frank told him.

It took a while for the corn field to dry out enough for them to start over. Frank felt bad too, remembering how those green leaves were just about three inches high when they were hammered into the ground. *I never before thought about the hazards and pitfalls of farming until now. It was a lot like playing Taroky for money and losing. Life wasn't fair.*

Thirty Seven

Frank remembered how his parents used to read the newspaper, *Bohemia*, that was a German newspaper published in Prague. The publications had notable contributors such as Franz Kafka. They liked keeping up to date on what the European governments were planning. Their discussion of what was being printed is partly why Frank wanted to come to America. It sounded like war was on the horizon, and he wanted no part of it.

Anton and Sylvia, likewise, kept up to date on current events nationally and globally. They were pleased to receive the first issue of *The Hospodar*, meaning *The Farmer,* which was now being published by the National Publishing Company out of Omaha, Nebraska. They got news of The Western Bohemian Fraternal Association (Z.C.B.J.). The Bohemians were willing to help one another and exchange work. The organization also offered insurance for the farmers. Anton mentioned to Sylvia that they might consider getting insurance against hail, but would need to discuss it some more and talk to others who had it. After the hailstorm they had gone through, it might be worth the peace of mind. And then, there were years, nothing like that happened. It was a gamble, just like farming.

Another newspaper that Anton and Sylvia read from cover to cover was *The Nebraska Farmer*. They liked reading about the going prices on crops. People they knew felt it was a reliable paper since it was started by the first settler to homestead property in 1863, even before the territory became a state.

Frank paid attention to the talk about prices falling and banks failing. Since they didn't have their money in a bank, they needn't worry that it affected them, yet, when prices fell, it affected everyone. He didn't exactly understand when they talked about The Sherman Act and about the government's involvement with purchasing silver.

Then it happened. In February of 1893, the new president, Grover Cleveland repealed the Sherman Silver Purchase Act, which created a panic and people rushed to their banks to withdraw their money. It was said that 500 banks across the country closed, thousands of businesses failed, and many farmers had to quit their operation. They read that President Cleveland borrowed $65 million in gold from the Wall Street banker, J.P. Morgan, along with the Rothschilds from England to shore up the country's gold standard.

Frank kept his ear to the ground to learn if there were any farmers near Brainard who lost their farms. He was old enough now to legally purchase property. On the first road north of Brainard and two miles east, just before Oak Creek in the Oak Creek Township, the Richardson property became available. It was the Southeast quarter of Section Nine in Township fourteen.

In the years Frank had worked for Anton and Sylvia, he had been able to save enough to pay cash for the property, but instead, he offered a sizeable down payment and became indebted to The Connecticut Mutual Insurance Company for the remainder. He would need to purchase farm equipment and livestock, so he chose to keep enough cash to get started.

Anton told Frank, "You have done well by us, so continue to stay and work for us as you gradually get your fields going."

"We all know that one hand washes the other, as they say, so I will accept your generous offer and continue to work for you."

Work he did! From sun up to sun down you could see that grey homburg he wore while working on his farm. He continued at Anton's seven days a week as well.

There was a spring-fed pond on the property where one could see Frank's red head bobbing up and down in the water when he needed cooling off. "This pond will keep me from having to dig a well right away as the cattle will have a place to drink fresh water," Frank said to Anton.

The next Sunday when he took a break to listen to the band at Old Man Tuba's, Frank said to accordion-man Joe, "I haven't done too badly, don't you think?"

"It's only been eight years, not?" Joe said.

"That's right. I'd like to let Uncle Thomas know that I have just about made my dream come true," he said. "I'm not through either. I hope to own the other quarter of the section one day as well."

Thirty Eight

What was nice about the post office box was that one could ride into town after the chores were done. Sometimes that would be around 8 o'clock in the evening during the summer. Supper was often eaten by candlelight since the men would work in the fields as long as it was light. Like other women of the day, Sylvia took care of the milking and tending to the other animals. Since it was customary to have leftovers from the noon meal for supper, it was mostly a matter of heating things up.

One evening, Frank bridled Noc and rode to town to get the mail. Kamos trotted along. It was beginning to get dark, but Frank could still see well enough to make out their box at the post office. The Farmer's Almanac was there along with a letter. He couldn't make out who it was addressed to or from, so it would have to wait until he was in the kitchen near the kerosene lamp that always sat in the middle of the table.

Frank dismounted, took Noc to the water tank for a drink and then led him to the barn, where he unbridled him. "Have a good night's rest, Old Boy," Frank said.

Taking his shoes off on the porch as he and Anton always did, Frank was eager to see if the letter might be for him. The envelope read:

> *Frank Lanc*
> *General Delivery*
> *Brainard, Nebraska*

"Who could be writing to me besides *Maminka?*" Frank asked the Houbovys.

"Well, open and it and see," Sylvia urged him, just as eager to see who it was from as he.

"It's from Josepha," Frank said. "As he read through the letter, a look of dismay covered his face.

"What is wrong?" Sylvia asked.

"My cousin Peter has been in an accident. We were like brothers."

"What happened?"

"Says here, he was thrown from a horse and had several broken bones and isn't healing like the doctor would like." After reading the letter over again, Frank said, "I must go see him. What if he were to die? I know it's a busy time of year, Anton, but do you think you can spare me for two or three days? I can take the train to Lincoln and then find a way to Brush Creek."

"We'll get by," Anton said.

Frank went up to his room and dug out the satchel he used when they came across country from New York. He packed a few things and set off to bed so he could get an early start in the morning. He couldn't leave his horse there while he was gone, so he would have to walk the two miles into town to catch the train. The whistle blew around nine each morning, and if he left at seven he'd make it okay.

"You're not going to walk," Sylvia said. "Anton and I are going to take you by wagon in the morning."

"The cows and chickens can't wait that long until you get back, and it's much too early before we leave to do chores. I'll make it okay," Frank told her.

It was a calm morning as Frank bid the Houbovys goodbye. The robins tugged at getting worms out of the ground as they chirped along the way. Frank had not slept well last night worrying about his cousin, hoping he would make it in time in case it was worse than the letter had indicated. What felt good to him was that he had the money for train fare to Lincoln. He wasn't sure how far Brush Creek was from there, but he would figure it out as he went.

Frank asked the ticket master for a round trip ticket from Brainard to Lincoln. The man told him the railroad charges two cents per mile. Brainard is 42 miles so that would be $1.68. Frank thought about asking if he could work for his passage, but thought better of it and decided that this time he would enjoy the ride and watch the scenery. He'd had his shoulder to the wheel ever since he left the old country. Now was a moment to sit back and reap the rewards of his labors.

"How far, Brush Creek?" he asked the conductor in his broken English.

"It's about 12 miles, I think, south of here," the conductor said.

Frank gathered up his satchel, put on his grey homburg, and set out walking south of Lincoln. He saw a sign that said Brush Creek and he set out walking. It was mid-morning. He should make it by evening. He met some farmers going into the city in their wagons. *Maybe one of them will be coming back before long and I can hitch a ride.*

He continued on foot down toward the direction of Brush Creek. He wasn't exactly sure where to find the Jelinek family, but calculated in his mind that someone would know where they lived if he ever encountered a single soul. He amused himself by studying the countryside, noticing who had fences and did not. The land was flatter than around Brainard. He remembered that his uncle liked to go for the very best. He looked at his pocket watch and saw it was 11 o'clock in the morning. Since the miles weren't marked off, he couldn't tell exactly how far he had walked already, but guessed that it would take him close to two or three o'clock to get to Brush Creek, unless, of course, he happened to be lucky enough to hitch a ride.

It must have not been his lucky day as no one came along and, he had estimated rather closely. When he arrived in the little town, Frank went directly to the bank figuring in his mind that if anyone knew where the Jelineks lived, the bank would.

It was a good assumption. The young man behind the teller's window asked Frank to wait. He went to another room and brought back with him a man wearing dress trousers and a satin vest over his white shirt.

"Good day, sir. My name is Frank Lanc and I have just walked from Lincoln to find my relatives, Thomas and Josepha Jelinek. Can you tell me how to find them?" he asked.

His English was much better by this time, but the banker was having difficulty understanding his thick accent. "Wait right here," the man said as he asked the young man at the teller's cage if he could help him out.

"This is Emil Jovak and he speaks Bohemian. Can you repeat what you just said?"

Frank obliged and Emil understood completely. He also could tell Frank where the family lived. "I go right by their place if you can wait until I get off work, I'll take you there," the young man said.

Frank nodded.

"Have you eaten today?" Emil asked.

Frank said, "Not since I left Brainard at nine o'clock. I could use something."

"You can get something at Sofia's Café down the street. Wait there and I'll come get you."

Frank found Sofia's place. He wasn't accustomed to eating out and felt rather awkward about what and how to even order.

"Can I help you?" the middle aged lady asked him.

"What's good here?" he asked.

"I have chicken and dumplings today for fifty cents," she told him.

"That's good," Frank replied.

When she brought him the food, she also brought him a glass of water. Frank grabbed the water and guzzled it down. Then he dug in as if he hadn't eaten for days. Sofia came by with a pitcher and refilled his glass. He wiped his plate clean with the biscuit and drank, yet another glass of water.

Mother Nature couldn't hold any more water, so he stood up. Sofia knew exactly what he was looking for. She pointed out the side door where he could find the facility.

Frank came back in and sat down at the table, but she had already cleared his plates and glass away.

In just a few minutes, Emil appeared at the door and spoke to Sofia.

Frank placed the fifty cent piece on the counter, said "*Děkuji,*" and walked out with Emil.

"I ride my horse to work each day. Do you think we can double up? I'll take you to their house. I hear their son had an accident," Emil said.

"That's why I came. I'm his cousin and I needed to see if I could cheer him up," Frank told Emil.

They rode what seemed like about two miles west of town when Emil stopped at the white, two story farmhouse.

"This is where they live?" Frank asked. He was somewhat impressed. Uncle had done well for himself in eight years.

"The bank owns this place and Thomas sharecrops it for them," Emil told him.

Frank was relieved knowing that it was taking Uncle Thomas just as long to get a foothold as it was everyone else.

"Thanks for giving me the ride," Frank said as he tipped his hat to him.

Thirty Nine

Aunt Josepha saw them ride up and stood on the porch with open arms. "It's so good to see you Franta," she said as she hugged him first on one shoulder then on the next. It will do Peter so much good to see you.

"How badly hurt is he?" Frank asked.

"The doctor says his body is healing well, but his spirits are low," Josepha said.

She led him to the bed they had put in the front room, so he could see the activity going on with his family. "Hello, Cuz," Frank said as he moved closer to him.

Peter's eyes grew brighter at the sight of his long lost cousin. "How did you ever find us?" he asked.

"I've never stop thinking about you and wondering how you were doing, and when the news came of your accident, my boss told me to take two days off to come to see you," Frank replied. "By the way, how do you like my American name, Frank?"

"Sounds good. Tell me all about what you have been up to and how things are going. Are you married yet?" Peter asked.

They reminisced and exchanged stories of what they have been doing the past eight years. They talked and laughed until the sun began to set. "Wait until my father sees you are here," Peter said and laughed.

Josepha purposely kept all the rest of the family out of the front room so the young men could talk. Rather than having left-overs, she went to the cellar and brought up a jar of canned meat (something always reserved for special guests). She knew Frank would be hungry after his journey.

Thomas came into the house to wash up for supper. He noticed there was an extra place at the table. He also noticed that she had set a place for Peter. He had not been joining them at meals. When the two cousins came into the room, Thomas almost fell to his knees.

"Franta, Franta, how are you, young man?"

"I'm fine and I'm hungry as usual," he said.

The children had all grown so much since they'd been apart, Frank hardly recognized them.

"Franta's new American name is Frank," Josepha told Thomas. He is now Cousin Frank to all you children.

They enjoyed a special reunion with many stories to exchange. It was the first time in several weeks that Peter seemed himself again.

"I would like to walk around the place and see what all is here," Frank said. "I was finally able to get a place because of a foreclosure due to the Panic. I have so much to do, to learn and to get before I can call myself a farmer."

"The Bank owns this, but we're renting and splitting 60/40," Thomas said. It is taking a while to save enough for land. I'm keeping my eyes open for a foreclosure too, but we like living here so well with the big house, we aren't in any hurry."

"What is that?" He pointed to the windmill.

"Come and I'll show you how it works. There is a well with a pump to get water out of the ground. Good tasting water, too. Then the wheel on the tower turns as the wind blows, it pumps the water into the tank for the cattle. Quite an invention!"

Frank was fascinated with the machine and said to his Uncle, "I'm going to make sure I have one of those in my yard."

The two had never talked like that before. Uncle Thomas was impressed with what a fine young man his nephew had grown to be. They went back up to the house as they all sat on the porch and talked some more.

"I have to start back early in the morning in order to catch the train back to Brainard," Frank announced.

"You don't have to walk this time as I am taking you back in the wagon. Your aunt has been wanting to go into Lincoln for some things, anyway, so that will work out well," Thomas said.

The cousins bid their farewells, and Frank headed back to his life in Brainard.

"We can't tell you how much it means to us that you came to see our son when he needed cheering up to help him heal," Josepha said with Thomas nodding in agreement.

Forty

By the time Frank arrived back in Brainard, he not only had worn a hole in the sole of his shoe, but the sole itself came loose and was flopping. Not wanting to spend money on a new pair of work shoes, he decided he would stop off at Old Man Tuba's to see if he could re-sole his shoes. It seemed to Frank that Tuba could fix just about anything. Tuba went out on the back porch and brought in a cast iron shoe stand and some shoe forms.

"I repair a lot of shoes for different folks," he said. "You came to the right place."

Frank watched as Mr. Tuba cut the old sole away from the heel and pulled out some new leather soles out of a box. He held the work shoe up to the light to see if they would need to replace the heels right away too, but told Frank that the heels could wait until another time. He found just the right size of sole and slipped the shoe over the shoe form as he steadied the stand between his knees. He began tapping nails around the edge carefully, so as not to pound it into the inside. Having nailed the sole down, he reached for his cutters and carefully trimmed away the excess leather. It was on to the next with the process repeated.

"How much do I owe you?" Frank asked.

"You don't owe me anything, young man. Just have me over for a good meal someday when you're married."

Whenever Frank was around Mr. Tuba, it felt to him like being around a grandpa. He slipped on the shoes, bid Mr. Tuba a grateful goodbye, and made his way back to Anton and Sylvia's.

It was mid-afternoon when he got there, and Anton was still in the field. It was too early to start milking, so he visited with Sylvia for a while telling her about his trip and visit, then stretched out on the ground, and took a nap. It had been a fast, physically draining, and emotional two days. He felt warm inside for going and seeing his cousin, along with his aunt and uncle and the rest of the kids. He couldn't get the image of the windmill from his mind. That would be something he would need to look into to see who could dig a well, put in a pump and windmill. He wondered how much it would cost him. Thoughts rolled through his mind as he lay there thinking of all there was he would need to start farming. His first priority would be building a house. Someone had told him you could order a house through the Sears & Roebuck catalog. It came by railroad, already cut to order with the instructions and blueprints. He assured himself he could do it since he had helped Anton and the neighbors build the barn.

He dreamed of having a house that faced east toward the morning sun. There he'd have a porch across the front. The back would be toward the west where he'd see the setting sun. It too, would have a porch that would be enclosed where they could store the milking equipment there and have a place for their work boots and overshoes. His wife would want to keep a tidy house. It would have an upstairs with rooms for their children. With his hat down over his eyes, Frank settled in for a good nap.

"Hey, Traveler," a voice shouted, waking him up.

Frank shrugged as he rolled over and sat there a while getting his bearings. He felt a little embarrassed for napping during the day, then said to Anton "The cows weren't ready for milking yet. I should have come out to the field."

"It's good that you got some rest after all those miles in such a short time," Anton said.

After chores were done and dinner was ready, Frank told the two all about his journey, his long walk, and how his uncle was finally over being mad at him.

Forty One

The days that followed were busy ones for Frank. His every thought was consumed by what he needed to do next in order to set up a farming operation. There was a small house that came with the land. Frank kept dreaming of building a Sears & Roebuck house kit when they became available.

There were plans for Brainard to build a flour mill like Ulysses had. Until such time, a small operation was set up so farmers could bring their wheat in and get it ground for flour. A local man ran this mill, and often you would find farmers lined up with their sacks of grain.

One such day, Frank rode Noc with a gunny sack full of grain over his neck, to the small mill. He hitched him to the post and took the bag from him. There was a bench to sit on. Frank went over.

"Fine morning," he said to the young man sitting in line.

"Mighty fine morning," the young man replied.

"I haven't seen you around. Are you new around these parts?" Frank asked.

"I'm Henry Topil. We live southeast of town half way between here and Loma."

"I've never been to Loma. It's not as big as Brainard, is it?"

"No it isn't, but it has a beautiful view of the valley below," Henry said.

"My name is Frank Lanc. I live a ways north of town with some folks that I work for."

"Did you come from Moravia?" Henry asked.

"No, I'm from Kladno, but I was born southeast of Prague in Castlava."

"How long have you been here?" Henry asked.

"I came with some relatives in 1885, but they settled in Saline County and I wanted to come to Brainard because of an ad I read in New York City. Do you have family?" Frank asked.

"There's my mother and father, Frank and Frantiska, and my sisters, Lena, Mary, Augusta and Clara. I was born in 1872. Lena is older, Mary is five years younger than me, and there are Augusta and Clara, both younger. So you see there is a bunch of us."

Frank was fascinated with Henry's large family and told him, "I was born in 1874, so we're only two years apart."

The two hit it off right from the start and time passed quickly as they waited for their wheat to be ground. When they got ready to leave, Henry said, to Frank, "You should come to our place for Sunday dinner one of these days."

"That would be mighty fine. Would two weeks from Sunday be enough time for them to get ready for me? I eat a lot," he said with a smile.

"I'm sure that will be good. I'll ask my mother if it's okay and if not, where can I find you?" Henry asked.

"You can leave a note on the bulletin board at the post office. I go there twice a week for mail."

Frank was pleased with his new acquaintance as he rode back with a sack of flour for Sylvia. While riding through town, he thought to himself that it would be good to see how Zenka was doing at the boarding house. He was happy, when he saw her taking sheets down from the clothes line, and he yelled out to her.

"Hey, Zenka. Remember me? Franta, Frank. I stayed with you a few years ago?"

"Sure, I remember you. How have you been?" talking with a clothes pin in her mouth.

"It's going fine for me. I've been working as a hired hand for Anton and Sylvia, where you told me to go. It worked out well. They needed someone and I have a place to stay." Frank said.

"I knew that their son had left home and figured they needed help. Have they ever heard from him?" she asked.

"Not that I know of, but I don't ask. By the way, I was able to buy some land by Oak Creek a little north and east of town. I hope to build a house on it someday, when some of the men have time to help me."

"That's great Frank. Thanks for stopping by. It's so good seeing you," Zenka said.

Forty Two

Most every Sunday afternoon the musicians gathered at Old Man Tuba's place for their polka fest. Frank joined in on his harmonica whenever they motioned him to. The time moved quickly as the men played, drank beer, and told jokes. The accordion player leaned in closer as if he was going to tell them a secret.

"I have to tell you about my father's neighbor who had a sow he needed to get bred. Since he didn't own a bore, he loaded her up in his wheelbarrow and wheeled her over to the neighbor's farm. He waited a few days and realized the mating didn't take hold, so a week or so later he put her in the wheelbarrow and wheeled her over there again. After the mating, he brought her home again. One morning the guy and his missus were eating breakfast. They looked out the kitchen window. There in the wheelbarrow sat the sow, ready to go again."

The men howled with laughter, slapping their knees. Frank laughed until tears rolled from his eyes. He wasn't used to hearing this kind of talk at Anton and Sylvia's. *It's good to get together with the menfolk and let loose,* he thought.

"Hey there, Frank, I told you I would show you how to make beer. Do you still want to know?" Tuba asked.

"Sure, but I can't do it at Anton's house. They don't drink liquor of any kind. I can learn and then wait until I move into my own place to make it," Frank said.

"It's gonna take some equipment like a boiling pot, a large glass bottle, a funnel, a bottle line bucket with a lid, a siphon hose—"

"Hold on, hold on, I don't have that kind of utensils. No use telling me how to make it until I can get my hands on the things I need to cook it with. Thanks anyway, though," Frank said.

On his way home Frank was thinking about where he would get hops. He would have to find out if Tuba grows them. For now, Frank decided he would rather grow poppy seeds like his mother did back in the old country. He could cultivate a patch on his own property. He really liked poppy seed *kolaches* and those poppy seed *buchty* like his mother used to make.

As he and Noc, with Kamos tagging along, made their way around the bend to home, he noticed some activity in Anton and Sylvia's yard. This was unusual. They seldom had visitors unless they invited them over. He approached slowly, not knowing what to expect. This was one time he wished he had a rifle with him just in case they were in some sort of danger. Frank dismounted at the end of the lane and began walking.

"It's okay, Frank. Ivan and a friend are here!" Anton called out to him.

That was strange, Frank thought. *He takes off – doesn't let his parents know where he's at and then years later just shows up again.*

Frank approached cautiously. Anton introduced Ivan and his friend to him. Frank tipped his hat. He felt awkward. Here he'd been staying in Ivan's room all this time. *Wonder if they are going to ask me to leave? Where's his friend going to stay? Will I still have work?* Frank decided to take it slowly. He would wait to have Anton tell him what to do. Frank led Noc over to the watering tank for a drink, led him into the barn, and headed toward the house. Sylvia was busy in the kitchen putting together some food. Frank walked in and gestured, "What's going on?"

"I'm letting his father handle this," she said.

"You and Anton need to let me know what I am to do now that he is back." Frank said.

Frank was quiet all through supper, letting the family talk. Ivan seemed friendly enough and talked as if he had been around forever.

"Rudolph and I are just passing through on our way to Canada. We thought we should stop in and see how the old man and old lady were doing."

Frank thought Ivan's reference to his parents was disrespectful, but didn't think he should comment.

"We're used to sleeping on the ground or the floor, so don't worry about where to put us, Ma," Ivan said.

Sylvia looked at Frank with a relieved expression on her face. "I let Frank have your room since you were gone so long. He's been our hired man for several years," Sylvia told him.

Frank was a bit uneasy that night knowing they were in the house. Again, he wished he had a rifle. He decided a man on the plains really needed some protection and that he would get one the next chance he had. In the meantime, he'd just sleep with one eye open.

Ivan and Rudolph stayed around for a few more days, not making any effort to move on. Frank took Anton aside and told him that he had made arrangements with Zenka to stay there until Ivan decided what was best for him, but that he would continue to come out to the farm and work unless Anton had different plans. Frank packed up his few belongings and went to the cellar to get his strong box with the cash. He continued to work for the Houbovys and collected his pay every Friday as before. After a few weeks, Frank was relieved when Ivan and Rudolph finally did move on to Canada.

Forty Three

It had been two weeks since Frank met Henry at the mill grinder. He kept checking the board at the post office and this day he saw the note:

> *Frank Lanc –*
> *Come for dinner this Sunday at 1:00 p.m.*
> *Henry.*

Frank's heart skipped a beat. He wasn't sure if Henry was serious about dinner or not, but here it was, an invitation.

The week lingered on forever until Sunday came. Frank told Zenka he wouldn't be at her boarding house to eat that day. Frank took his straight edge razor and sharpened it on the strap, then went out to the back porch where Zenka kept a basin and mirror. He carefully shaved his stubbly reddish-brown beard, slicked back his hair and wearing his cleanest shirt and overalls, he headed south toward the end of town and then east three miles on Noc. He left Kamos with Zenka for the day.

The Topil family welcomed him like he was a long lost relative. Henry's parents held out their arms for handshakes with both hands. The dining room was set with lovely dishes which he noticed had roses on them. Standing alongside the table were Henry's four sisters. They were all pretty, but Frank noticed Mary right off. She was the prettiest of them all, all five foot two inches of her, with long, dark brown hair and hazel eyes. She had her hair pulled back with some sort of a clip holding it away from her face. What fascinated him most is that she had earrings in her earlobes. He had not seen that ever before. The other sisters didn't have pierced ears. They smiled politely as everyone sat down.

"My wife always wants to say a blessing" Mr. Topil said.

They all crossed themselves and as soon as they said Grace, Mrs. Topil and the girls got up to get the food from the kitchen. It looked and smelled delicious. They passed the pork roast, dumplings, and sauerkraut. Henry handed Frank freshly baked crescent rolls. Frank was in his element. Sylvia was a good cook, but this was what he remembered bohemian cooking was supposed to taste like. They ate and chatted, mostly just getting acquainted. As they finished, the girls took the plates into the kitchen and Mary came out with dessert. Frank could scarcely believe his eyes. As her skirt brushed his shoulder, she handed him the plate with *buchty* on it.

"I have been dreaming of *buchty* ever since I left Bohemia. My mother always made them," Frank said with a gleam in his eyes.

Mary was smiling, pleased that he would enjoy them. "They are filled with poppy seed filling that I mix with egg and raisins."

"You made these, Mary?" Frank said. "They are as good as *Maminka* used to make."

After dinner, the men went out on the porch to talk while the women did the dishes. Frank stayed until 4:30 p.m. hoping he wasn't overstaying his welcome.

That night as he lay in bed and thought over the events of the day, he said to himself, "That Mary is the girl I'm going to ask to marry me."

Frank continued to visit the Topil family on Sundays and even on warm summer evenings. One such evening, on his birthday, August 8, after Mary served them a plateful of freshly baked blue plum *kolaches*, Frank asked her if she would like to have a ride with him on Noc. He helped her up on the horse and then hopped on behind. Noc looked back to see what was going on with the extra weight on his back, but gently they walked down the long lane and along the side of the road. It was a beautiful evening as they rode toward the setting sun. Frank was trying to get up enough nerve to ask Mary for her hand in marriage. He smelled the fragrance of her hair and he stopped the horse.

"Mary, I've been wondering about something. Would you be interested in being my wife?"

Mary smiled at him and said, "I would need to talk to my parents about that first. I will have to let you know."

At least she didn't say no. He knew by the way she looked at him that she liked him as much as he liked her. And she made those *buchty*.

The next time Frank rode out to the Topil place, Mary came running down the lane to greet him. "They said you would make a fine husband and you already have land and a house. There is one thing, though, I want to wait until next June to get married."

Frank couldn't contain his joy any longer. He picked her up and twirled her around then kissed her on the lips. He wondered how he could contain himself for ten months. He would just have to bury himself in his work.

Forty Four

There was much to be done to ready his farm for a wife. While working for Anton so he could have an income, Frank spent every evening until almost dark doing what he could so his bride would be happy with their new home. He was able to find a used brass bed at a farm sale. He decided he would order a mattress from Sears & Roebuck catalog. He heard they were making cotton filled mattresses instead of ones made of straw. Another item Frank would buy for Mary would be a Hoosier cabinet. He saw one in the catalog at the Post Office. It was about two feet deep on the bottom part and shallower on top. The top part had shelves for dishes along with a flour bin and sifter on the left side. It sat on casters so it could be moved around the kitchen. The one he chose was painted white with colorful tulips painted on the doors. He was sure she would like it. He would keep his eyes open for a set of dishes. He wanted her to have some that had roses painted on them. He remembered that her mother had some like it.

As the months rolled by, Frank never missed a farm sale. Then he learned that a local farmer was selling out and moving to town. The man was sickly and couldn't work as hard as was called for in the fields. That was where Frank was able to round up most of the equipment he needed to start planting in the spring.

Frank spent the few spare hours he had with Mary at her parent's place. While the weather was nice, they took horseback rides in the area enjoying the beautiful countryside. Both of them liked the outdoors, as one would have to in order to be farmers.

"When we live on our place, do you think we could plant some fruit trees? I would like a blue plum, an apple, and a cherry tree," she told Frank.

"I don't know much about planting fruit trees," Frank said.

"I will save the plum pits and apple seeds from our trees. We can get the cherry pits next spring. I'll take care of that part if you will help me plant them," she said.

Mary's sisters would giggle when Frank was around and then tease her when he left. She ignored them. Mary had a lovely disposition – even tempered and jolly.

Forty Five

It was a beautiful summer morning as Frank prepared to go after his bride, Mary Topil, in order to travel to David City, Nebraska, for their marriage. Frank had purchased the train tickets. Mary was doubly excited since she had never ridden on the train before.

The plan was they would be married before Judge Hale in the County Court on Monday, June 28, 1897. Mary would have liked a church wedding, but no churches in the area had been built yet then. Her brother, Henry, would travel with them and he would be their witness. They would leave around 9:00 a.m. which would put them into David City easily by 10:00 a.m. They would walk to the Court House and wait for the Judge to become available. After the ceremony, they would walk to the Boston Studio to have their wedding picture taken.

The Boston Studio provided a variety of wedding attire since most settlers were too prudent to use their precious funds for clothing they would only wear once at the most. The studio provided a suit with vest, shirt, and tie for Frank. Mary chose to wear a long, light colored dress with puffy sleeves with a collar that had bobbles and a tie. She wore her dark hair flat to her head and pulled back into a bun. They stood in front of an ornate bench.

Mr. and Mrs. Frank Lanc, the 23-year-old groom and his 19-year-old bride, along with her brother Henry, caught the train on its way back to Brainard where her parents, Frank and Frantiska Topil had a lovely celebratory meal waiting for them.

Frank and Mary arrived at their own home by a horse-drawn wagon. Frank helped Mary descend from the wagon and led her to the front door of the small house. He hoisted her into his arms and carried her across the threshold. Mary's eyes opened wide when she saw the lovely Hoosier cabinet along with a table and chairs and the iron wood-range.

"You have done well for yourself, Frank Lanc, – in just these few short years since you came to America," Mary said to him as she turned and kissed him.

"One day soon, my *Laska*, I will build you a bigger house where we can raise our children and we can use this one for a summer kitchen," Frank told her.

Together they watched the sunset as they sat on the porch and listened to the gentle sound of water flowing through Oak Creek that ran through their property.

Afterword

Grandpa Frank achieved his dream of owning land in Butler County, Nebraska, in Oak Creek Township 14, slightly north and two miles east of Brainard, Nebraska. A few years later, he and my Grandma Mary purchased adjoining property to increase their land ownership to one half section totaling 320 acres.

They gave life to nine children: Joseph, Madeline (my mother), James, Edward, Helena, Verona, Jacob, Laura and Frederick. Many, many other descendants, such as myself, owe our lives to their existence.

Legend has it that Grandma Mary, who was born in Butler County Nebraska between Brainard and Loma, survived the flu pandemic of 1918 due to the tender loving care of my mother. Madeline, who at the age of 18, nursed Grandma Mary to recovery by her prolific use of garlic soup, and garlic poultices.

When Grandpa was 44 years of age, he registered for the World War I draft and at the age of 48, he filed for the Declaration of Intent for Naturalization. Grandpa realized another dream when all of his sons played musical instruments in various bands in the area.

There is an old Czech adage that says: Every Czech is a Musician.

Upon their retirement from farming, my grandparents moved from the home place to an acreage in a southwest section of Brainard, along with Grandma's dog, Pupina. There Grandpa raised tobacco and Grandma grew a large vegetable garden.

As a youngster, I remember when all their sons gathered there with their musical instruments. Along with a friend named Joe, and his accordion, they made that little house rock with their music.

Frank Lanc passed away at the age of 77 on April 28, 1952. Mary Lanc passed away on December 2, 1966 at the age of 89.

Frank and Mary Lanc on their wedding day
June 28, 1897

Frank and Mary Lanc on their 50th wedding anniversary
June 28, 1947

Appreciation

My heartfelt appreciation goes to my husband Bob for his interest in the story; to my family for their encouragement; to my sister Helen Alfrey for stories of her recollection of our Grandfather; to Carolyn Dvorak, who lives in Brainard, and without whose research, I would have not been able to document places and locations; to Sharon Bruner, Brainard historian, who was the first person I spoke to in Brainard, for information; to my cousin Richard Lanc and his wife Nancy, who helped inspire me to put our memories on paper; to Leonard DeWisplare for help with family research; to my cousin Kathleen Reed for adding to the stories from our childhood with our grandparents; to Troy Seate for encouraging me to get published; to my writers' group, who gave me constructive feedback whenever I asked for it; to cousin Henry J. Topil for his ancestry information; to Suzana Ashworth for her translation of a document; to my friend Nancy Roeder, who recommended my publisher; to Angela Keane, my wonderful publisher; and to Patricia Cox, whose keen eyes worked diligently to correct anything I may have overlooked. Without them, my story could not have been possible.

About the Author

Adella Pospisil Schulz is a Nebraska native who has spent all of her adult life in Colorado. She is married and the mother of four grown sons, three daughters-in-law, seven grandchildren, five great grandchildren and six great, great grandchildren. Her passion for writing began in a one-room school house in elementary school and has remained with her throughout her life. Upon retiring from ten years with an airline, running a bed and breakfast for five years and owning her own fingernail boutique, she published a memoir of her own life story, *Adelka: Memoirs of Adella Pospisil Schulz* as well as her husband's life story, *The Life Story of Robert Lee*

Schulz, a cookbook called *Sweet Adeline's: Collection of Czech Recipes*, and a children's book called *My Nine Lives: The Life Story of Tony, an Amazing Cat*. She has had numerous short stories published in various publications and newspapers.